WHOSE BABY IS IT?

Reverse Harem BWWM Mafia Romance

Jolie Damman

CONTENTS

CHAPTER 1

Orena

My heart was pounding, more so than it ever did in any other situation I was in before. I was waiting for them to come. Who were they going to be? I didn't know, but I was waiting for them nonetheless. I had to admit that I was so nervous I thought I was going to be biting my own nails, but time was passing and I was already sweating less.

I looked at my watch on my wrist, wondering when they were going to come. When my 'friends' suggested that I should come to this blind date with three distinct men, I didn't think I was going to find myself at this rundown building. Not only was it the kind of place where I would never go unless someone pointed a gun at my head, it was also located on the outskirts of the city, where nobody dared come to.

I took a deep breath, finding pride in the reflection I saw in the mirror. It was my reflection, highlighting the curves of my body. I was seated on a single chair in the middle of the room. Scanning my surroundings, I noticed that it didn't have much in terms of furniture. Certainly not much more than a bed, the chair where I was seated on, and a dresser. I didn't dare to open one of its drawers, fearing that a cockroach would come jumping out of it.

I knew that my fears weren't baseless. I'd seen a cockroach when I was climbing the stairs to the room.

The clerk at the front desk, a scrawny and short man who couldn't be more than 20 years old, had regarded me with judging eyes. For him, it was quite curious that a woman like me, who looked imperious and ready to take on the world, had come to this dump.

But enough was enough about that. I didn't want to feel narcissistic or that I had too high of an opinion about myself. That wasn't the case at all.

This was a different type of hotel, where privacy was always kept at a maximum. I didn't even know the name of the clerk, who didn't have a pin on his chest. To be honest with myself, the mere looks of the clerk disgusted me. When was the last time he took a shower?

The stench that was coming from him… It was something I was forever going to remember, and it didn't matter how hard I tried to erase it.

When I dreamed about my types of men, I dreamed of hunky, powerful white bosses claiming me, doing whatever they wanted to me, and finally taking my precious virginity. I knew that it was something that would eventually happen, especially now that I was in college, but it was difficult for me to wait, regardless. Actually, for me, it was a lot more than that.

Whenever I was with my 'friends' and they boasted about what their first times were like, I felt ashamed of myself. They always boasted about how much pleasure they brought to their pairs, and I craved doing the same. That was why I was so nervous right now, wringing my hands.

It didn't matter how hard I told myself that everything was going to be okay, I wasn't going to know that for sure unless the men I was waiting for were in the room with me.

Before arriving here, I took care of myself, combed my hair, sprayed perfume over my body, and made sure that I shaved my pussy. The last thing I wanted, when the time was right, was to disappoint my dates.

It's what this was. Nothing more than a one-night stand with three men who were more than willing to share me.

As for them, they were going to come, but it was going to take a while.

They were men used to doing whatever and everything they wanted to their partners. They knew they were commanding, influential studs who didn't wait before doing everything they could to stake their claim.

I stood up, beelining to the window, where I pushed up the segmented curtain, revealing what was outside. It was as if everything terrible that could happen outside was. Criminals, drug addicts, whores, and the like were outside, polluting the streets.

I wanted nothing more than to be far away from them. It was such a pity that the men that I matched with said that they were going to come, but that the place they had to go to had to be here. I tried, thanks to the privacy that the phone app provided me with, to convince them to go elsewhere, perhaps one of the luxurious hotels downtown, but they didn't budge.

I tried to tell them that I was uncomfortable coming here, but I gave up on that. The blind date was one of the most memorable events in my life. So much so that I was betting everything I had that I was going to lose my virginity here.

As if to show that my coming here wasn't a waste of time – and if it was, I would be disappointed that I had come all the way here for nothing – three cars pulled over by the building. Three men slid out of them, dressed in dark suits as if this was a business meeting.

That couldn't be the case. I was impressed by who they were or, at least, who they appeared to be. They looked so much like businessmen I wondered if my initial assumption was wrong. What if they were around here for something else? Perhaps they weren't even going to come up to the floor where I was, but I was clinging to hope nonetheless.

A moment later, when I perceived that they were coming toward the building, my heart started to race. It was as though I was going to have a heart attack. It was finally going to happen, wasn't it? I still struggled to come to terms that I had to put myself in this kind of situation.

I was going to have to lose my virginity to three men, and they were handsome and excessively sexy. My eyesight wasn't as good as it was when I was younger, but when I spotted them from afar, I knew that they were a sight for sore eyes. Sharp hair, flawless jawline, dark sunglasses, and beard still to be made.

The confidence with which they carried themselves was unmatched. I wondered again if I was going to disappoint them, but then I realized that it was too late to be fearing that. The three businessmen-looking 'partners' just stepped inside the building, and I knew that they were going to come for me.

A second later, I realized that they were chatting with the front desk clerk. I couldn't make out the words, but hearing their voices… I knew that they were different. They weren't just mundane, boring white men that had come to pop my cherry, but rather men from outside the country.

The thought that I was going to have my first time with foreigners was thrilling. Out of all my friends, none of them had sex with a foreigner and now I was going to do that with three of them.

I paced around in the room, wondering if this was some kind of mistake.

What if they were going to kidnap me? What if they were going to do unspeakable things to me and I could do nothing but scream for help over and over again? It was a possibility, but one I didn't want to entertain right now.

After all, the decision had already been set in stone and whatever was going to ensue here, I had to go through with it.

I fished out my phone, dialing my friend's number. I wasn't going to call her, but I was going to shoot her a message, saying that it was finally going to happen.

I also mentioned that I was scared that something dreadful was going to take place, but I didn't dive too deep into the details. After all, I didn't want to scare off my best friend.

I put the phone back on my chair where I had been seated not too long ago. Looking back at it, I wondered if it wasn't possible to just make everything go back to what it was like.

I took another look in the mirror, checking myself out one more time. Adjusting my clothes, it wasn't that I felt insecure about my body, but about my big nose. It was just too big. So much so that when the 'businessmen' were in the room, it was one of the first things about me they were probably going to notice. Although, I had to admit that, if that happened, they probably weren't boyfriend material, not that I was thinking I had to date them more times beyond this afternoon.

I peered outside, realizing that none of the businessmen from before had gone elsewhere. Time passed and I could only think that this was taking too long. So much so that I just wanted to be with the businessmen as soon as I could.

Still pacing around in the room, I jerked when the door started to creak open. It wasn't that they were breaking into the room, but that they knew I had to be here. It was what the app mentioned to them, and they were eager to find out what their partner looked like in person.

But as for them, they probably weren't too happy that they were going to have to share me, I soon realized after noticing the glares they were giving each other. They thought that they were going to be able to do that, but soon realized they couldn't.

I didn't want to think that something wrong was going on here, but the look in their eyes was telling. It was as if sparkles of electricity were flying between them, showing that they were ready to fight each other if it came to that.

But as for me, I just wanted this moment to be over as soon as possible. Not the part regarding our sex, but the one that came before it – where they mulled over the possibility of opening fire.

They were still stepping into the room and I couldn't see what they were hiding in their suits, but men like them had to have guns with them. And not just guns, but they also came with bucket loads of bodyguards. They were men who didn't play around with their safety.

"Hi…" I stammered, trying to break the ice between us, but it was difficult doing so. Now that I was finally with my dates, I had no idea how I was supposed to react.

They finished stepping inside the room, studying me with their eyes. What was going on in their minds, I had no idea, but it had to be something good and vile at the same time.

They weren't just looking at me – they were dissecting me with them, confirming that they came here only for me. They wanted every part of me, to love me in ways I never thought possible, and to make me their black queen.

"Hi," one of the 'businessmen' teased, his voice husky and throaty. It was over-the-top sexy, but also foreign-like, just like I knew it was. They were perfect the way they were, looking as if they were over 30. The age gap was significant, but it wasn't a turn-off. Quite the contrary, in fact. It made this much better. Much spicier, I corrected myself.

CHAPTER 2

Gildo

One would think that my name had something to do with my personality, but it didn't. I was Gildo. Just that. Nothing more than that, and also a menace to people who crossed me.

It wasn't a dream what I was doing here, but it was something I wanted. It was a pity that I had to be doing it with two of my enemies, but this was also just a coincidence. I didn't think I was going to come across them and that we were all going to be in the same shitty room, but that happened and so here I was.

Nevertheless, I couldn't care less about that. What I was obsessed with was the beautiful woman standing across from me. She looked out of place, being in this rundown building that just wasn't for her. I couldn't say this to her right now, but she deserved to be in a mansion, a place where she could have everything and anything she wanted.

The only problem with that was that this was nothing more than a one-night stand. I had to keep that in mind, unless I wanted part of my life to come crashing down on my head. It wasn't going to happen. I wasn't going to let it.

Now, I wasn't going to let the uniqueness of this moment shackle me. Thinking that, I started to unbutton my suit, removing it. I removed the top part of it, chucking it over my head. I had no idea how we were going to go about this, but I was taking the initiative nonetheless. I had to. It was the only way. I was immensely competitive and I always wanted to show my enemies that I was on top.

Silvio grunted, but didn't say anything. Good. He could become my cuck.

I stepped toward Orena. I knew that was her name and I wasn't going to pretend otherwise. She made herself look smaller than she was, but that was okay. I knew that my presence was unnerving. That was the reason why she was stepping away from me, even though it wasn't going to do her any good.

If anything, seeing what she was doing, I was already feeling a little exasperated.

"I guess there's no point in saying what we came here to do," I affirmed, feeling that my voice grew thicker and deeper.

She shook her head, arguing, "Wait. Let's stop and think about this."

I approached her, pushing her up against the wall. My enemies were still taking off their clothes, and they weren't going to dare to stand between me and my black queen. I knew that it was sudden, that I shouldn't be thinking that way about her, but it was difficult not to. Her hair, her nose, and pretty much everything about her were just impeccable.

Moving my fingers between the strands of her hair, I could feel just how soft and weightless it was. Orena was paralyzed, wishing to do unspeakable things with me.

"What do you want to talk about?" I hissed, for a moment realizing that my enemies were still in the room, but it was also as if they weren't. It was just me and Orena, and she was still conflicted. I had no idea what she was thinking, but it was clear that she was afflicted. The way her chest was expanding and contracting told me so.

And I couldn't have that. I wanted her to be willing. She also said in the app that she wanted to do this without protection. We were both tested before coming here and so we knew we could do it.

In the meantime, the only problem was that she was putting her hand against my chest, showing me that she didn't want this to go on. It would be a huge disappointment if it didn't, and so I was hoping she was going to change her mind.

"It's happening too fast."

Really? That was unacceptable for someone who came out hunting for a date with three Italians.

"How old are you?" I asked, looking into her eyes and admiring their beauty. Her cheeks made me want to brush my hand over them, to feel the softness of her skin, and I knew she was thinking the same thing. She had to be. Orena was like that, I could tell.

If there was one thing that my enemies feared about me, it was how easy I could read people.

"21…" She responded and then gulped, making me tilt up my chin. A 10-year age gap wasn't that significant – at least not for me. I had been with younger girls aged 18 to 20, so I knew that it was daunting. It was much more than that, in fact. They wanted to be with me up until the point when they realized that they had never been in such a situation.

"You don't need to worry. Don't worry about the age gap. It's not important to me, and what is that one thing that people always say, anyway? That age is just a number?" I asked, not knowing how she was going to take that.

But then, when I realized that she began to unbutton her shirt, I noticed that she wasn't thinking about that anymore. I felt a hand appearing out of nowhere, moving me away from her. It was Silvio, who also wanted a piece of her, but I wasn't going to let that happen. As soon as I took a step back from where I was, I pushed him away with force, but not to the point where we started a war between our families. We were both in the cocaine business, making heaps of money from it.

Everything needed to remain okay between us after today.

After all, this was nothing more than an experiment. It was just a one-night stand where we were going to have a good time, and nothing more than that.

What was happening here, all of us meeting up in a rundown building where anything and everything could happen, was just a coincidence. So much so that, the coming morning, when I remembered this, I'd ask myself if I hit my head.

I groaned, showing my mug to Silvio. He didn't show that he was afraid of me, but he wasn't going to overstep our boundaries, I presumed. We were enemies who were going to share the same woman, but we were going to be respectful.

I grabbed her, took her to the king-sized bed in the room, and laid her down on it. Her eyes wide and paralyzed, she couldn't even blink. I started to lower Orena's pants, loving how smooth her skin was. I could be touching it for all of eternity, and it was a pity that I couldn't.

She shivered, closing her eyes when her pussy was exposed. It was shaved and almost entirely pure, untouched. Gleaming under the dimmed sunlight, I knew she was wet and about to have an orgasm, even though not much had happened yet. The innocence I could perceive in her eyes was telling. This wasn't just a moment where she felt uncomfortable, but it was also when she presumed she was going to lose her virginity. I didn't have to look at my enemies' eyes to know that they were thinking the same thing, too.

Even Adamo had the same gleam in his eyes, that perception of deep understanding. He'd finished taking off his clothes, stroking his dick now. He was thinking the same thing, wasn't he? He craved breeding her, to turn her into his little plaything, and Orena was more than willing.

I groaned. Fuck. I couldn't let my enemies take advantage of her. I knew that they were both obsessed over the same thing. They were going to use and discard her, and do no more than that. The coming morning, she'd wake up in this room and speculate over what even happened. I couldn't let that follow its course.

That was a weakness of mine. I showed compassion far too

often, far too many times, and it was creeping out right now as well.

"Fuck, you're so gorgeous. I love your smell, your perfume, the way the light bounces off your skin. Everything about it is as if it was made for me," I hissed, not thinking about anything that didn't involve pleasing Orena in all the ways conceivable.

And so, not wasting any time with that, I thrust my tongue out, flicking it up and down against her clit. It was engorged, pointing at me, begging to be worshiped. I was doing a lot more than those things and I knew that my plus-sized queen was okay with that. So much so that she gripped the bedsheets tightly, making it hopeless for me to even consider stopping what I was doing.

One lick after the other, I showered so much pleasure on her she couldn't even breathe properly anymore. Seeing that she was suffering so much, I stopped what I was doing, letting her bask in the shockwaves of pleasure.

When Orena was back to being her normal self again, I asked, "How are you feeling right now?"

"Like I don't want this to end any moment soon," she replied, throwing her legs around me and shoving me down again. Licking her clit several more times, I wasn't surprised when I felt the mattress sagging. Silvio was climbing up the bed, easing himself between her and me. Pumping his dick, he pressed his fingers to her lips, parting them.

In no time at all, he maneuvered his prick between her wet lips, moving it up and down, fucking her mouth. I wasn't going to say that I admired what he was doing or what my eyes were witnessing right now, but I wasn't going to deny how hot it was.

Gosh, Orena was losing herself, gripping the bedsheets so tightly thanks to the way I loved her clit. After one last lick, I wrapped my fingers around my prick, noticing that she was ready.

I wasn't going to cuddle or worship other parts of her skin more than I already was. This wasn't about that, after all. It was about nothing more than fulfilling a wish of mine, and it was happening. I was horny, hard, and my dick was enraged. I was going to penetrate her.

Adamo positioned himself by Orena's side, lowering his head when he realized that he was left with just one thing – or two of them, actually. Her boobs. They looked delicious and succulent, even from afar. The hardness of her nipples didn't lie about her intentions right now. Orena wanted to be where she was, to be doing the things she was right now, and we were giving her everything she wanted.

I couldn't hide the smile that crept up on my face when I moved closer to her, taking in the sight of her shaved and soaked pussy before easing my dick inside of her. I stretched her walls and she bucked, clenching them around my dick.

While Adamo mauled on her boobs, she was going to milk my shaft. Lovely. And I was going to be the one taking her virginity, too, which was just breathtaking. I was already on the verge of exploding and erupting even though not much happened yet, and I could tell that my enemies thought the same thing, too.

Gosh, Orena was so tight. Was there any reason to think that this shouldn't go on until I was creaming inside of her?

CHAPTER 3

I was inside her mouth, sliding up and down slowly, taking my time. The look on her face was enlightening. She was enjoying every second of what we were doing, taking this to level 100 from the start. Her mouth was burning hot, wet, clenching around my shaft. The more I fucked it, the more I felt like I was in control of everything.

I continued my movements, rolling my hips. I was aware that Adamo was right behind me, mauling on her boobs. I could hear the wet, rubbery sounds that he made with his mouth. I didn't have to peek behind my shoulder to know that he was adoring Orena. And he should be. After all, she was exquisite, delicious in every way I could imagine she was.

Just ravaging her mouth wasn't sufficient for me. I needed more. Coming to that conclusion, I started to roam my hands around her body, feeling the softness and smoothness of her skin. It was the color of chocolate and I could imagine that the taste was dangerously similar, if not better, too.

Given my position, I couldn't move freely, not without hitting Adamo and I didn't want my butt to go up against his face. That would be *weird*, not to mention a huge turnoff. Thinking that, I decided to do better for Orena another way.

I had no idea if she was ready for it, but I started to pick up the pace, but without taking it to a level too high. After all, it would be a huge turnoff for her if I started to pound in and out of her mouth without giving her enough time to recompose herself.

Sweat pooling on her forehead, she could barely think that this evening she was going to find herself in this room, being devoured by three men at the same time.

Likewise, I didn't think she was going to be so stunning. I wanted to cream inside of her, and I knew that Gildo was already doing that. I could tell that from how loud he was moaning right now, groaning when he hit his orgasm.

Goddamnit. I didn't want to think about it this way, but I was far too competitive. He was *creaming* inside her pussy, tainting her womb. It wasn't going to be the same when it was my turn. I wasn't going to be the one who took her virginity and that pissed me off.

Deciding to push that thought out of my mind, I pumped up my pace moments later, only making sure that I wasn't deep-throating her. I wasn't, which was a relief. There were still so many inches that could go in, but right now they weren't going to. Given the look on her face, the sweat on her forehead, and the color of her cheeks, I could tell that she was really having enough already.

After all, she was being pleased by three men at the same time, enjoying every little bit of it.

My balls were tight and I could feel that my climax was about to come. When it was, it would flare up in my body, engulfing every part of it. It was strenuous to control myself, my body growing warmer by the second. My entire focus was on her, on creaming inside her mouth. Orena was begging for that, I could tell. The way she glided her hands around my body, cupping my asscheeks so that I was even deeper inside of her was enlightening and also rewarding.

I decided not to waste any time, groaning when I felt that her fingers were sneaking between my asscheeks. It was a line that she shouldn't cross, and she took that hint moments later, realizing that my ass was reserved for my wife. I didn't come here with my ring and Orena was never going to find out about that part of my life.

Retreating her hands from my ass, I increased my pace just a little bit more, so that I was ravaging her mouth even more roughly than before. Orena was basking in every moment of it and was begging for me to cream inside of her mouth.

I was no coward and I wasn't going to back down, proceeding all the way in when the time was right. Moments later, I started to cream inside her mouth and I could tell that she enjoyed the salty taste. Orena wanted even more of it, clenching her lips around my shaft tighter than before. As the seconds ticked by, I knew that it was time to pull out, but I didn't want to. I didn't want to ruin the moment.

And so, my eruption went on for what appeared to be minutes. Scratch that, I reprimanded myself. It went on for what felt like hours and I could tell that Orena was going to walk out of here without feeling hungry. She was going to feel no hunger and to-morrow morning she was going to wake up feeling sated.

My balls rested on her chin when I decided to pull out pain-fully slowly. She fought against it, but it was pointless. Whatever I wanted to do to her, I was always going to. After all, she was the submissive one and I was the dominant Alpha, even among my enemies. I never thought the first time we were going to bond, that it was going to be with a woman. I always imagined that we were going to go to one of the soccer fields downtown to compete in a little match.

Orena seized my ballsack, but it was too late. What surprised me was that she finally cracked open her eyes, gazing at me and holding me with her eyes. I thought it was impossible, but I could see that she was different. She was a plus-sized, black queen, but still very much different from any woman I had been with, includ-ing my wife.

I groaned again, not even wanting to think about my wife right now. She didn't deserve to be in my thoughts, especially after everything she spewed to my face. She was considering taking my kids with her, and I wasn't going to let her. I wasn't going to kill her, but I was going to do something that was going to make her think at least three times about her delusion.

I caressed her forehead before murmuring, "I'm going to be back, baby. You don't need to worry about that and… I've got to say that you were amazing. You are amazing."

She smiled shyly, showing me that she enjoyed my compliment, but that that was that. We were having nothing more than a one-night stand and things were going to remain that way. It was a shame that I was probably not going to see her again, but that was the way our lives were.

Still slowly pulling out of her, I wasted no time before replacing my enemy that was behind her fanny. He didn't give me a second look, instead opting to take my place in front of her mouth.

I didn't look at his cock, but I could tell that it was already getting soft. He came inside of her, which was something I loathed. I was going to have to share the same place where he was, where his seed was, and there was nothing that could be done about that, unless I wanted to step out of here thinking that he was going to be the one who gave her a baby.

I mean, chances were it wasn't going to happen, but we could never be sure. Nevertheless, if Orena wanted to try her luck, she could. She could fool all three of us, making us think that she was pregnant. Things would go to another level of heat if she was. I didn't even want to think about the possibility of that playing out. If my wife found out about this, things would go downhill in my house, even more so than they already were.

Adamo was happy mauling on her boobs, enjoying every inch of them. He even pinched her nipples every so often, making her arch her back.

Her body was covered in sweat, her chocolate color now looking a little more crimson.

I took pleasure in what my eyes were devouring, finally stepping between her legs. They were perfect, the curves flawless, the weight just right. I held her thighs with confidence and without digging my fingers into her skin. She knew where I was, but it was as though I wasn't there.

Keeping that in mind, I dipped my head, sticking my tongue out. I closed my eyes and took in the smell of her pussy. As I basked in it, I felt how intoxicating it was, enjoying every moment of it.

"How the hell did you stay virgin this whole time?" I murmured to myself, truly finding that intriguing. She either had strict parents or she'd been saving herself up for the right man. Whatever was the case, I wasn't going to bring it up now. The only thing that mattered at the moment was pleasing myself and having a moment I would never forget.

I started to lick up and down her snatch, enjoying every moment of it. The skin was exquisitely soft and smooth, as if she had never been touched, even though I knew that wasn't the truth. Gildo had been inside of her and I would never forgive him for that. I never could.

A couple more licks after the first few and I could tell she was ready. Interestingly, I didn't feel the taste of Gildo's sperm. I had no idea if it was just my mind blocking it, but it was my perception.

Her snatch pulsed, begging me to come inside of her.

I pouted, kissing her snatch. As I played with her folds, she started to shiver, her whole body trembling. As this moment dragged on, I could hear the groans and moans around me from my enemies. We weren't going to try to kill each other or anything like that right now, but I still had to be alert. I still took all the necessary precautions when I came here, after all.

Deciding to waste no more time, even though the taste of her cunt was liberating, I grabbed her thighs again and pulled her to me slightly so that I didn't bother the other guys.

After this was done and our next meeting, we weren't going to be able to look at each other with the same eyes. We just saw each other naked and it was a memory that was forever going to remain in my mind.

Seconds later, I started to play with her tunnel, teasing her. I was teasing Orena that I was going to break in right now, but I didn't. I liked toying with my food and that was the way things were, at least for me.

When I was finally done and tired of that, I breached her pussy's folds, going all the way in. Gosh, she was still so tight, I noticed, picking up the pace soon after. I was aware that I had just come inside her mouth, but my balls were still heavy with the rest of my milk and I could orgasm again, no doubt.

I groaned when it finally happened, painting her pussy with my semen. Her body trembled, her pussy clenched tight around my shaft, and I knew that she was having another climax. The way she reacted, her fingers digging deeper into Gildo's back was exhilarating, almost as good as the way I came inside her tunnel.

Slowly, but surely, I eased myself out, loving the way that a rope of my come was attached between my mushroom-shaped head and her folds.

It was finally disconnected when I took a step backward, thinking that this was ending and I had to put my clothes on.

I hated that, but I had to go back to my wife. After all, she and the kids awaited me.

CHAPTER 4

Adamo

The night I had with Orena was going to forever be in my mind, and I didn't think I could keep pretending that my fiancée was still enough for me. She was seated on my lap, rubbing her ass against my crotch, but it wasn't sufficient. She cradled her phone in her hands, flipping different marriage proposals and decorations.

I didn't have time for that right now, my mind going back to when I also took Orena's virginity. Gildo was the first one that claimed her flower, but I was the first inside her pretty, chocolate-like asshole, and I could feel as if I was still inside of it. I came in there and then inside her womb, feeling how perfect and tight it was. Nothing was quite like a woman, especially a black princess like her, losing her virginity…

"So, what do you think of this one?" Magda asked, showing me a couple of beautiful bouquets, but I could do nothing more than groan gently and study them for a couple of seconds. After all, I had to keep pretending that I enjoyed her company, even though that wasn't true anymore. I liked her company before, when she wasn't so focused on losing weight. I swear, nothing was worse than her thinking that she wasn't shaped like a model. When was she going to realize that she was perfect the way she was – or had been, to be more precise?

I still thought that I was going to marry Magda, but I'd lost the original appetite and I didn't think I was going to reclaim it.

"Adamo?" She asked, barely aware of the fact that we were both in my house, surrounded by piles upon piles of bodyguards. They kept the place protected and it couldn't be any different. Far too many enemies sought to kill me, including those that I found in that rundown building. Still couldn't believe that that place was the only one we had when we chose the address for the date.

"It's pretty and I like it," I replied, feeling like a needle just pierced my heart. Lying in my line of business was an essential skill, but I didn't enjoy lying to my fiancée, especially when she was still… mostly friendly and caring. She always did everything that was asked of her, including being on my lap, like she was right now.

She was compact and petite, the perfect size for someone like her. Still, my hands wanted something bigger and more succulent to grab on to right now.

Someone on the outside would look at me and judge me, saying that I was being heartless, but they didn't know anything about me. At my age, I was already thinking about settling down, having two boys, just like Silvio. And also, hopefully, to not end up like him, with a wife that didn't like me and having to care for kids that preferred being with his spouse instead. At least, that's what I thought.

"You're not paying any attention to what I'm saying," she whined, pushing herself off my lap and then landing on the other seat of the couch. Across from us was a huge TV, playing a series that I couldn't care less about. The reason for that was pretty simple, of course. I still thought of Orena, her ass going up and down on my shaft, making me feel like I was 18 and losing my virginity all over again. It was a silly thought, but one that was in my mind, and I couldn't shake it off.

Magda pursed her lips, looking like a whiny brat right now. That was one more thing about Magda I didn't like much, even though her personality hadn't changed much from the person she used to be. Still pretty sweet, playful, cheerful, and that kind of thing. She was such an angel and I couldn't help but feel that I was being a little too harsh on her right now. Maybe even a little selfish.

When the spark of a relationship ended, not much could be done to rekindle it, wasn't that right? It was something that my grandfather once told me a long time ago, when he noticed that I was already 13 and growing taller than him. He groomed me to replace my father and that I did, earning the rank of boss in my mafia family in record time.

More like our narcotic mafia family, I remembered. Nothing quite like hiding from the authorities and making heaps of money while doing so. It was one of the reasons why I enjoyed my 'job' and why I would never leave it.

"Darling, I was paying attention to everything, I swear," I affirmed, putting my arms around her, only to find her shoving her shoulder against me and then jumping off the couch.

What the fuck? I thought, finding that flabbergasting. Did she think that she could just hit me like that in my own house? My anger rising in my heart, I couldn't help but shoot up from the couch as well, towering over her.

"No, you weren't," she cried, spinning around and then running up the stairs, going somewhere I couldn't even try to figure out right now. When she was pissed about something and wanted to puff out of existence, she could do that like a professional.

I didn't think much of it, just coming to terms with the fact that our relationship had turned sour and that I couldn't do much about it. It wasn't that I was thinking about going back to Orena and that we were going to have an amazing life together, but that I was pondering finding someone else that wasn't Magda or Orena.

Regardless, it was best to hit the bar, and that I did, stepping outside the house and going to my limousine. One of the drivers was already outside as he wondered what was going on. After all, it was probably the first time in his life that he was seeing me so pissed off. I was huffing. It was one thing having an argument with my girlfriend and another to see her doing what she did. We were still going to talk about it, but I was pissed. I wanted nothing more than to forget it all and to grow a backbone. I should tell her, as soon as I came back from the bar, that we were going to break up. No more marriage.

"Boss, do you want me to take you somewhere?" He asked, already opening the door of the limousine, which was by the front of the mansion.

I nodded and replied. "Take me to the bar, and you know which one I'm talking about. I don't need to spell it to you."

"Right away, sir," he said, sitting down behind the steering wheel. I sat behind him, in the other compartment of the limousine, and soon the vehicle was driving out of the property.

I paid little attention to the buildings and the houses going past us, focusing my attention on what words I was going to use when I was back. Magda was still someone I was fond of, even though I didn't think we were going to marry. Didn't think? I was certain of that.

In the meantime, my mind went back to Orena. That night I had with her, even though I had to share her with the other guys, was forever going to remain in my mind and there was nothing I could do about that. Was it possible to find someone like her? I didn't know and I wasn't hopeful about that.

"Boss, if you don't mind, do you mind if I ask-" he was saying, but I cut him short by saying, "Yes, I do mind. You don't need to know anything about it."

He was going to ask me about the breakup, but I didn't have the patience to talk to anyone about it right now. He was only acting that way because he wanted to become one of my friends. Every time he took me somewhere, he always initiated a conversation, and now was no different.

I closed my eyes, forgetting that I was inside the limo when, minutes later, it halted. I wasn't paying attention to the road, and I realized that it was too soon. We shouldn't have already gotten to the bar, right?

Of course not.

I reopened my eyes, finding out that a familiar figure was stumbling along the sidewalk. I closed and reopened my eyes, thinking that it just couldn't be true. That incredible woman from that night couldn't be there. It just didn't make any sense.

A woman like her was probably in her bedroom right now, or seated on her couch, sipping from one of the most expensive wines in the world. Why would she be outside when it was dark and gloomy, when she had no one to protect her? After all, even though she was a virgin when we met her, I was pretty sure that now she was already with someone who cared about her, who loved her, and who was going to do everything in his power to keep her protected. At least, that's what I'd do.

My eyes studied what they were seeing more closely, my mind making out what could be the only solution to the puzzle. It was her. It was Orena and I couldn't believe it. My heart raced, more so than it ever did before in my life. I had no idea why I felt this way about her, but there was no denying that the feeling was in my heart and I couldn't shake it off.

"Stop the car."

"What?" Thomas asked, turning his head around so that he was gawking at me. He was so surprised that I was asking him to pull over in what appeared to be the middle of nowhere, where all the houses and the buildings had their lights turned off.

"Pull over. There's someone I need to talk to right now," I warned, locking my eyes with his. It took him no more than a fraction of a second to realize that I was serious. He pulled over and I jumped out of the limo, noticing that Orena was still stumbling.

And I just realized that her belly was bigger now than it was when we met. She was a bigger girl that night, but her belly was still different this time. It was as though she was pregnant, which could have happened, but it also couldn't have been because of us, right? It just wouldn't make any sense. She promised that she was going to take all the precautions so that she didn't get knocked up.

At least, that's what she promised. But now that I was thinking better about it, what if she decided to take advantage of that opportunity to get a baby?

It was impossible. It didn't make any sense and she would get nothing out of that. If she was thinking that she could blackmail us by having one of our babies, it just wasn't going to work. Blackmail didn't work on us.

I sped up to her, putting my hand on her shoulder. I realized that calling her out wasn't going to work. It was as if she was drunk.

When she turned around to meet me and I felt the stench coming out of her mouth, I knew that that was the case. She was drunk and was probably so for a couple of hours already, given how disoriented she seemed. She was still plus-sized, just like she was before the night when we met her, but she looked weaker. Feebler, almost as if she hadn't been eating well for the past few weeks, or even months.

"Orena? What happened?" I asked, feeling something for her I could only describe as the seed of love. I had felt it before when I first met Magda. Or perhaps was just feeling sorry for Orena. It was difficult to figure out what was going on in my mind, especially right at this moment when so many things were popping up in it.

For a few seconds, Orena didn't say anything, just standing there, looking as if she was going to fall over on the ground and start to cry and bawl her eyes out. Hoping she wasn't going to do that, I readied myself for anything that could happen. I was here, ready to put my arms around her and to keep her close to me.

I was a protector like that. When I felt sorry for someone, I was always ready to keep them protected. It was one of the reasons why, I supposed, I always wanted to have children.

"I just lost everything," she cried, throwing her arms around me and hugging me tightly. It happened out of nowhere, but I was ready for it. I could only hug her back, putting my arms confidently around her. She was warm, though not as warm as when I met her that night. Whatever happened to her, it really destroyed her. Her mind was shattered.

I let her cry in my chest for the next two minutes, nothing of importance happening around us. It was as though no one lived nearby, which couldn't be the case. People lived in this part of town. I was certain of that.

Nevertheless, if other people were watching us right now, I didn't care. The only thing I cared about was making sure that Orena realized she could trust me. She could rely on me to help her out right now. I had such a soft, gentle heart when it came to women, I thought.

When she lifted her head, she opened her mouth to say something to me, but I lifted my finger and pointed it to the limo. "Let's go somewhere warmer, where you'll feel more comfortable. And don't worry about the driver. You can tell me everything you want and he'll keep his lips sealed."

She nodded once, still holding on to me as we made our way to the limo. I held the door open for her, helped her sit down in the seat, and then strapped on her safety belt.

After doing that, I opened the door on the other side and sat down by her side. Waving my hand, I informed the driver, "Just drive and take me to a hotel. It doesn't matter which one, as long as it is good."

He opened his mouth as if he was going to say something to me, but then he realized that I didn't want to make conversation right now, and especially not with him. The limousine started, driving across the streets. In no time at all, it was as though nothing of what happened before did. Nevertheless, Orena was still right here by my side, tears coming out.

"You can tell me everything that happened. I know that this is only the second time we are meeting, but I want to show my support. I just can't see a girl like you suffering at night, in the middle of nowhere."

She bit her bottom lip, wondering if she should spill out everything.

A moment later, when I wondered if she was even going to say anything, she replied, "I really just lost everything."

"What do you mean about that? What did you lose?"

"They came for my mother. They killed her in front of me, and now I have no one. My mother was the only thing I still had."

I clenched my hand. I didn't think that it was that terrible, that she just went through something so horrible. Who could kill someone's mother like that? I didn't know, but I was already promising myself this – I was going to avenge her.

"Who did it?" I asked, realizing that the first question I should be making, even though it didn't pop up in my mind before, was why they wanted her dead.

She shook her head, avoiding my eyes. When we met that night, she never did that, which showed me that what happened utterly destroyed her mind. She wasn't the same person as before. She wasn't as strong-willed anymore.

"I don't know. Everything is still such a mystery to me."

I looked down, finding her belly as I wondered if I should make one more question that just popped up in my mind. Instead, I decided to ask another one.

"Why did they want to kill her? I mean, was she someone special?"

She shook her head again, replying, "I don't know. It happened out of nowhere, when we were watching TV in the living room. I just managed to escape, and I don't even know how I did. It was a huge group of them, men in dark suits, almost as if they were assassins. I guess that someone put a price on my head."

I ruminated on what she just said, making the following plan in my mind - I was going to take her to an apartment, pay for it for as long as she needed, and, in the meantime, I was going to hunt down whoever put a hit on her head.

It was going to take a lot of time and perhaps I was even meddling with stuff I shouldn't get myself involved with, but it was worth it. If I just abandoned her, I would feel as if I was betraying myself, and I couldn't let that happen.

"Don't worry about it. I'm going to keep you safe."

"Really?" She asked, turning her eyes to look at me. Despite her weakness and the stench coming out of her mouth, she was still the same stunning woman from before. I wanted to kiss her, to make out with her, but I couldn't. I would only be taking advantage of her, which was something I couldn't do.

It was for that reason that I felt relieved when the limo was parked inside the parking space under the building.

CHAPTER 5

Orena

The apartment where I was living now was better than my house. The truth was that, even though I liked to look that I was richer and more well-off than most people, I wasn't. I was dumb, poor, and now things were even worse, for someone had put a hit on my head and I had no idea who it even was. All I knew was that I was being hunted.

I just walked out of the bathroom when I heard someone knocking on the door. It could be only one person, remembering that said person was none other than Adamo. I couldn't look straight at his face without remembering all the things we did that night.

He was helping me now, paying for this apartment, and I felt bad about it. For one, I didn't think I deserved it. I was hiding something from him that I shouldn't. He made no questions about it so far, but I was pretty sure he wasn't stupid and that he knew something was up. And second and last, he came here often to check up on me, which was more than anyone ever did before.

"Coming," I announced, beelining to the door and opening it. Adamo was nothing short of stunning. He came here dressed with a plain button-up t-shirt, office pants, boots, his beard made, and his hair shining under the light of the candelabrum.

And, in his hand, I noticed that he held a box of chocolates.

It was shaped like a diamond and it looked heavy. Taking another glance at it, I realized that it contained chocolates of several colors and flavors.

I wasn't stupid, realizing that he came here with second intentions. But now that I was feeling better and I knew that he could keep me protected, I welcomed him. There was no point in doing the opposite, after all.

"Adamo. It's such a surprise to see you here," I said, opening a half-smile.

Adamo smiled too, showing me his perfect teeth again. What we did that night when we had that one-night stand was forever going to remain in my mind, tainting whatever relationship I could have with him. So much so that I couldn't even look at him romantically.

"I just thought I should check up on you," he said, his lips looking so pretty, so inviting, making me want to kiss them right away. It was such a pity that I couldn't. At least, I knew that I shouldn't. I fell in love once with someone that never knew I was in love with him and, if there was one thing I promised myself since then, it was that I would never allow the same to happen again.

"Thanks. That's so kind of you," I said, inviting him in and closing the door behind me. When it was just the two of us, even though I knew that guards were posted outside the apartment building, I felt compelled to do things I never would otherwise. And one of those was letting whatever was happening here come to fruition. I was going to play along with his plans.

"It's nothing. I just brought you something. I hope you like it," he said and then we went to the kitchen island, which was right across from the living room. It took him no more than a couple seconds to get there. He deposited the box of chocolates on top of it, opening it.

From where I was, I could already spot the different smells of the chocolates. They were enticing, making my stomach rumble even though I ate not too long ago. I didn't like boasting about it, but I was a good cook. It was one of the things that impeded me from falling into depression when it hit me hard once.

"It looks really nice," I said, picking up one of the chocolates. I threw it into my mouth, started to chew it, and then swallowed it after savoring its taste for what felt like minutes.

In the meantime, Adamo watched me, paying attention to every movement I made. There was no denying that he had a crush on me and it was difficult for me to figure out why. After all, I didn't look like my normal self anymore. I felt better, but I didn't frequent the gym anymore, didn't cook often – certainly not as often as I would like – and I always cried, especially every time I remembered that my mother was dead and that I could do nothing about it. Even the rest of my family thought that I was dead or had disappeared.

I couldn't call anyone, couldn't talk to anybody. Adamo said that that was for my own protection and I believed him, but it was still such a hard pill to swallow.

Adamo popped one of the chocolates into his mouth, chewing it slowly as his eyes locked with mine. My breathing was quickening, realizing that he was checking me out from bottom to top. His eyes followed the definition of my curves, the cleavage on my chest, and the shape of my lips. He wanted all of me. He wanted everything and couldn't be stopped.

"I know it's been a while, but I think it's about time you told me exactly what happened after that night."

I didn't have to ask him which night he meant. Adamo was talking about the night when I lost my virginity and everything changed. It was the day after that night when I noticed that people started to follow me, taking notes on everything I did. It creeped me out, made me call the police and tell them what was happening, but it was too late and they didn't do anything about it. They could be involved, but I didn't give that possibility much consideration. After all, it helped me with nothing.

"I'm not so sure I'm ready for that," I admitted, swallowing down another chocolate. The taste was as good as the first one, the flavor slightly different, but I wasn't paying much attention to it. My eyes were focused on the man standing across from me, his expression telling me everything. He was determined to find out the truth and I couldn't keep it hidden from him for much longer.

"I can't wait much longer. If I'm going to help you find out who killed your mother, then you need to tell me everything."

His voice was deep, exuding his determination. I took a deep breath in, walked away from the box of chocolates, and wrapped my arms around my torso. It was my way to keep myself protected or, at least, to feel that I was slightly safe right now.

"I'm still thinking about it."

Adamo closed the box of chocolates and I heard his footsteps approaching me. When he was behind me, he settled his hand on my shoulder, and it was warm and comforting. I knew that he was trying to give me confidence, and it was working.

"They didn't come just for you, did they? They didn't want to kill your mother. They came for something that's inside of you," he affirmed, his eyes on me.

I spun around, meeting his eyes. I knew what that meant. I knew what he implied and there was no point in pretending otherwise.

He retreated his hand, letting it fall to the side of his body.

"You don't need to keep it hidden from me anymore. I know what happened."

Adamo knew what happened. Everything had been such a whirlwind since that night in that rundown building that I didn't have time to take the needed precautions so that I didn't get pregnant. But it happened and now I was pregnant with their baby, or babies.

I didn't even have time to go to the doctor to be certain. All I knew was that my belly was growing bigger by the week.

"Why didn't you tell me anything about it until now?" He asked, standing uncomfortably close to me. I knew that he wasn't going to try anything, but he was doing everything in his power to make me tell the truth.

I looked down, avoiding his eyes. It was as if they were looking right into my soul. I couldn't hide the truth from him and I wasn't going to try, anyway.

"I felt ashamed of it. I feel ashamed of myself. I was so worried, so busy with other things I didn't do the only thing I was supposed to."

"There's no need to feel ashamed of it and you shouldn't, anyway. We took a risk and that's it. I only wonder if there is just one baby, then whose baby is it?"

I looked up, feeling like I wasn't even in my body anymore. I staggered over to the couch, sat down on it heavily, and then buried my face in my hands. I wanted the floor to open up and swallow me whole.

"I don't know and I don't want to think about it anymore. I fear that if the other ones found out about this, they'd try to kill me, too. And even though I don't even know what being a mother will be like, I want it to happen. I want to be a mother, to care for my baby, and this is the opportunity I'd always been waiting for."

Adamo sat by my side more comfortably and gently than I did, putting his hands on his lap. I knew he was looking at me. I could feel his eyes on me even though I wasn't looking at him.

"Running away from it or trying to won't help you. You need to face the truth, go see a doctor, and then we can figure out what to do after that."

"I don't have money for that. I can't even work or go outside."

"You don't need to worry about that. You don't need to concern yourself with money. I can pay for everything, if it means digging out the truth."

And in the meantime, I couldn't wrap my head around the fact that everything changed so much since that night. It was only supposed to be a one-night stand. I shouldn't have gotten pregnant. It shouldn't have happened, but here I was now.

I turned my head, meeting his eyes one more time. It was difficult not to feel that we were creating a strong bond when he was being so caring and loving with me. I felt that he just might be the one who I should settle down with.

He settled his arm over my shoulders, dipping his head slowly. *It was going to happen.* We were going to kiss and then everything would change. I would have to live with him for the rest of my life, and I wanted that. If there was someone I wanted to be with, that person was him.

But then I pushed myself away from Adamo at the same moment, shooting up from the couch.

"I'm sorry," I said, racing over to my bedroom and shutting the door behind me.

What was I even doing? Was I going to fall in love with Adamo?

CHAPTER 6

Gildo

"**Y**ou're telling me she's with him?" I asked, raising my voice. I couldn't believe what my lackey had just informed me about, his hand holding his phone and showing me several photos that he took of them. I kept tabs on Adamo and Silvio, and it shocked me that the first was with Orena. I still thought of her, thought of the amazing night we shared, and I couldn't believe that asshole decided to go after her.

I felt jealous and possessive. I couldn't let him have her, no matter what. Thankfully, I didn't have a fiancée or a wife and didn't have to explain my intentions to anyone.

I was in my Ferrari, seated behind the steering wheel. I'd come here to the outskirts of the city for a meeting, but my mind was, right now, focused on something else. I was focused on finding out what Adamo thought he was doing. Did he think that I was going to let something like that slide?

It was a good thing that he was coming here – or should already be in the office. After the meeting with Silvio, I was going to tell him everything. He was going to be pissed that I kept tabs on him, but it wasn't like it was a secret, anyway. After all, he kept tabs on me, too. Things were like that in the mafia underworld and nothing was going to change.

"Yes, sir. Looks like he took her into his limo, and then I don't know where he went with her. Do you think he took her to his home?"

I scratched my chin, weighing that possibility. "It's possible, but I don't think he did. When did you say this happened?"

"No more than a couple of weeks ago," he responded and I felt my hand clenching. She was a good girl, Orena. Younger than me, perfect, pretty, and lust-inducing. Even just thinking about her right now, all I wanted was to get her out of wherever she was. I was going to dig out the truth, no matter the consequences.

"If you don't mind, I'd advise that you don't do anything too rash during the meeting. It would be better if Silvio didn't suspect anything," my lackey said and I held his gaze, tipping up my chin.

"You know I can't do something like that. I'm going to dig the truth out of him, one way or another. I thought that he was a man of his word. We all agreed that, after that night, we weren't going to keep in touch with Orena. We couldn't."

"I don't like where this is going," he lamented, showing me a couple more photos, making my blood boil. She wasn't just with him. They sat down inside his limo and then… I didn't know what happened then, but it couldn't have been anything good.

"I don't need your permission to do what's right," I insisted, noticing that, in one of the photos, her belly seemed bigger. Initially, I didn't think much of it, but now I realized that it could mean something I didn't even want to entertain right now. What if she was pregnant? I mean, did she even want to be pregnant with my baby?

Or the thought that the baby was Silvio's or Adamo's… I didn't even want to think about that possibility, shunning it.

"It's time to go up there," I announced, opening the door of the Ferrari and sliding out of it. I adjusted my tie, my guards following me, and then we went to the elevator. Wally pressed the button, taking us to the last floor of the building. The office was located in the section of the building where we could see all of downtown, and I was a little relieved that Adamo wasn't here yet.

Not even Silvio. Those assholes thought that they could keep me hanging here or something like that? If that was the case, they were soon going to realize that I wasn't someone who showed forgiveness often, especially when it came to their lack of punctuality.

I sat down, interlaced my fingers, and settled my elbows on the long and round table. I then closed my eyes, waiting for time to pass and, after what felt like no time at all, the door opened.

It was Silvio. Good. At least he didn't waste any time coming here. As for Adamo... who knew what he was doing right now. Probably taking advantage of Orena, something that he should be feeling deeply ashamed about. Not that I thought he could – just that he should be feeling that way.

"Silvio, it's good that you've come here on time."

"I never arrive late for anything, always at the right time," he joked, cracking open a smile, but I didn't retribute. I didn't like smiling when it didn't mean anything, and why would I have smiled right now anyway? It wouldn't have achieved anything.

He sat down, saying, "Looks like Adamo is late. I wonder why..."

"I wonder the same too, though I might have a pretty good guess on why he is," I confessed, leaning back on the chair and meeting his eyes again. He raised one of his eyebrows, but didn't say anything. He knew that I was hiding something, but was going to wait until the right time to say anything about that.

"You're being cryptic all of a sudden, and I don't like it," he grumbled when the door opened and Gildo stepped in. He didn't have a smile on his face, but the hickey under the collar of his shirt... I knew that it meant something, and it made my blood boil. Now... it was probably from his fiancée, but I started to think that it was Orena's and coming to that conclusion hurt me. What if he already had enough time to soften her heart and convince her that he was the one who deserved being with her?

I couldn't have that.

When Silvio stepped out of the office, I shut the door, putting myself between it and Adamo. He narrowed his eyes slightly, glaring at me. We were alone. Not even our bodyguards were here with us.

I needed to be alone with him to dig out the truth.

"Gildo, what do you think you're doing? I don't like your attitude."

I waved my hand, dismissing his concern. "I didn't come here to start a war with you and it won't happen. There's just something I need to discuss with you in private."

"In private? What do you mean? We couldn't discuss it with Silvio?" He asked, keeping his distance. He was a fearless man, but he wasn't going to do anything that might come off as a threat.

"I'm not going to dance around it, so I'm just going to say that I'm disappointed. I saw you with Orena. I know that she's living with you."

His expression didn't show anything distinct, but his fingers twitched. He knew that I was aware of what he did, and it was something he didn't expect from me. He thought he was so smart, always keeping everything he did hidden from everyone.

But that night, when he went outside without better preparations, he made himself vulnerable.

"How do you know? Were you keeping tabs on me? Was someone you ordered following me?" He asked, but there was no need to answer it. Yes, I was following him, keeping tabs on him, and it was no surprise.

"Answer my question."

Silence hung in the air and I wondered if he was going to spill out the truth. If he didn't, I wouldn't let him out of the room. He wasn't going to walk out of here without telling me everything he knew and did.

"It's none of your business. She was just a girl that we met, that we fucked, and that's that. There's nothing more to it than that."

"Obviously, she's a lot more to you. She's living with you now, isn't she?" My voice was deep, throaty even. I was going to get the truth out of him and was going to do everything in my power to achieve that.

He stepped away from me, wandering to the huge window facing the outside of the building. It was raining outside, the water drops battering against the glass panel.

When a slap of thunder streaked across the sky, he confessed, "I saved her. After that night, I saved her. She needed me."

"What are you talking about?" I growled, keeping my distance. Going anywhere near him wasn't safe, especially when he was pissed.

"Someone's hunting her down and she needs our help now more than ever. I mean, she needs *my* help. As far as I'm concerned, you could be the one who put a price on her head."

"I did no such thing. I would never. She's just a civilian and that's all she is."

"I'm not so sure about that. I know about the things you did, the things you do when people aren't looking and when you know that the authorities will ignore you."

"You know nothing about me."

"If you say so, but if you're thinking that I'm going to let you anywhere near her, then think better about it. I won't. I'm working on finding out who is trying to kill her, and I can't trust you now."

"I didn't even say that I want to see her."

"You shouldn't have said anything. You should have kept your knowledge about us hidden. It's not going to help you. In fact, it only makes things worse. Now I know that I need to be more careful even when you aren't around."

I opened my mouth to rebuke him, but it was pointless.

"Now, if you don't mind, I need to go out. And don't follow me like you did last time. I won't be as forgiving again."

I should've done something, but I couldn't. He cornered me,

making it so I couldn't even say anything else. He knew that I was aware he was with Orena, and he was in the right. Even though I still had strong feelings for her, we didn't have anything in common, and that was that.

He went to the door, opened it, and halted. I wondered if he was going to say anything, but then he didn't. He just walked out, leaving me completely alone. Well, not completely alone, for Wally just stepped back into the office, but it wasn't like I could discuss with him what transpired.

"Boss?" He squeaked, trying to draw my attention to him, but it was pointless. I was staring at nowhere in particular, thinking. I had to come up with a plan. It was going to hurt, but there was no other choice. It was the only way to see Orena one more time, even though she was supposed to mean nothing to me. After all, she was nothing more than a girl that we fucked, just like he said.

I clenched my hand, rushing out with Wally as we stepped outside. He held the Ferrari's door open for me, even though he didn't need to. He was a good guy in his early 20s who tried hard to impress me. I could give him compliments right now, but I didn't. My mind was busy with something else and that was Orena.

I needed to figure out what to do about her.

CHAPTER 7

Silvio

That bitch. She got pregnant, hid it from us, and was now under Adamo's care. She thought that that was enough, that he was going to keep her protected, but things weren't so simple. So much so that I was already planning on meeting up with her, especially now that Gildo also knew the truth.

I didn't care if my wife found out about us, but if the truth came out, my kids would certainly learn everything and that was something I just couldn't have. I couldn't disappoint them. They were the only thing keeping me sane right now.

As I thought that, they both hurried to me, giggling and smiling broadly. "Oh, look at how much you've grown up," I said, patting Quinto on his head. He couldn't contain his smile, hugging me tightly when he realized that it was no mirage. I was here and I was hugging him back, wishing that nothing else was happening right now. I was free and happy with him, and he was one of the most important people in my life right now.

I broke the hug, moving so that I could hug his brother. Bonifacio buried his head in my chest, stammering as he said, "Daddy, I'm so happy you're back. I thought I wasn't going to see you again until the weekend."

And it was so shitty that our lives had to be this way. Nothing was going my way, especially in my line of work. Now that the threat of Orena being pregnant loomed on the horizon, I wished for nothing more than to pretend it was a dream. A terrible, heart-wrenching nightmare, but nothing more than that.

I looked up, realizing that my wife was in the living room, perched on the couch and thumbing the screen of her phone. She didn't even look up to acknowledge my presence. I couldn't wait until she was out of the house and never had to see her again.

"Come on. I'm going to be here a while, so off you go. I bought you something, and it's in the backyard."

Their eyes lit up and then they headed off to the back of the house, disappearing. When I couldn't hear them anymore, loneliness struck my heart. Without those two sugar plums keeping me company, it was as if I didn't have anyone I could rely on.

And now that I was thinking about it, I really didn't have anyone, did I? I didn't want to admit it, but living for so long with a wife that I didn't like and couldn't stand, I felt suffocated. I had trust issues now, which were gobbling me up from the inside out.

Deciding that my life needed a thunderous change, I went to the kitchen and closed my eyes. The kitchen was such a perfect place for reflecting, which was what I was doing right now. I needed to meet up with Orena, but how? The more I thought about it, the stronger I concluded that it was impossible, but not without starting a war, and that wasn't something I could afford right now.

Just when I was beginning to lose hope, someone showed up in the kitchen. For a moment, I thought that it was my wife, but then I realized that it was someone different. One of my men, much older than me and with hair already going gray. He had a different look on his face, as if he was about to tell me searing news.

Some of my men knew about the mission which was attempted not too long ago. We tried to kill Orena, but it didn't work. I had no idea how she pulled that off, but she did and was still alive. How that happened was still a mystery to me and it was going to remain that way for the time being.

I just needed to find out if the baby was mine. I still couldn't believe that she didn't abort it when she found out about the pregnancy. What a bitch. I had no idea what she was planning on doing with the baby, but I couldn't allow it to come out. If the baby was mine, it couldn't live.

"Boss, I think I've got something you want to know. It's about Orena."

I stood up right away, my attention fully focused on what he had to say. If it was about that whore, then I needed to know everything.

"I sure as hell hope you're going to tell me you've got something that can actually help me."

"We just found out that she has a phone number. This is it."

He handed me a piece of paper that had a string of numbers. It had to be her phone number, which was a great find. I looked up, finding his eyes and pulling up the sides of my mouth.

"You did an amazing job. Expect a raise soon," I said, turning around with the piece of paper in my hand. I walked out of the house, went to the left, where I could have some privacy, and then pulled out my phone. I dialed her number, hoping that she was going to pick up soon, but then all I heard was static.

What the hell? I asked myself, wondering what was going on right now. My soldier couldn't have been confused about it. After all, he depended on me, depended on me thinking that he deserved his raise.

No matter, I thought, trying to decide how I was going to punish him when, all of a sudden, I heard a woman's voice from the other side of the call. I was already ready to end the call, but now I realized that I almost made a mistake.

"Who's this?" Orena asked and, for a moment, I remembered what she was like. I remembered the amazing moment we had together, wondering if it was possible to experience it all again. I didn't think it was, so I didn't build false hope in my mind right now.

"Orena…" I growled, wondering what her facial expression was like right now. She had to be surprised, after all. I doubted she knew that I was the one who put a price on her head, but she still had to be astounded that I managed to find her number. I truly needed to give my subordinate a raise.

"Silvio?" She asked, almost sounding too surprised.

"Surprised? Do you happen to have something you want to tell me?" I asked, baiting her to tell me about the pregnancy. She had to. After all, I deserved to know if I was the father or not. And if I was, then my children could never find out about it.

"How did you get this number?" She asked. Her voice was suddenly much weaker, almost as if she really knew that the baby was mine and that she should have aborted.

"Is that important?"

"It is. I just changed my number recently."

"Are you with Adamo?"

A moment of silence, nothing more than breathing coming through the other end of the call.

"Why do you want to know? You shouldn't have anything else to do with me and you really don't. I'm nothing more than a stranger to you, just like I was when we met."

"You're so audacious. You think you can do anything, especially now that you think you are pregnant with my baby."

Another moment of silence, nothing coming through the call.

"I don't think we should continue this conversation."

"I know you are with Adamo. I know that you are living together. Do you have feelings for him? Do you know that he's already with someone else?"

She stammered, but still responded, "I knew about that."

"You didn't. That's a lie. Let me tell you this one thing before you try to end the call – I'm not someone you can lie to. I always know when someone is lying, and I knew you lied to me when you said that you aren't pregnant. Why did you hide the pregnancy this whole time? Why didn't you abort?"

Another moment of tension. If I was in front of her right now, I would be pinning her against the wall, showing her that I wasn't kidding about what I was saying. I wanted to know the truth and she was going to give it to me.

"I don't even know how you know that I'm pregnant."

"Answer my other question."

"I don't have to. Adamo is keeping me safe and that won't change. If you want to do something about that, you should talk to him."

"You're braver than I thought you were, or maybe just stupid."

Heavy breathing from the other end of the call.

"I'm going to end the call now."

Just when I was going to say one more thing to her, the line died and all I could hear was more static.

I knew she was going to do that, so I wasn't pissed. More disappointed than that, I thought, turning off the screen of the phone and staring at nowhere in particular.

I shoved the phone back into the pocket of my pants when Bonifacio and Quinto showed up all of a sudden, hopping around me.

"Daddy! Daddy! We know," they shouted over and over, almost making me suspect that they overheard the conversation even though it couldn't be the case. They were sweet, innocent beings that could never do something like that. Not without regretting the same moment they tried to.

I picked up Bonifacio, spinning around with him like he was a baby all over again. Seeing the broad smile on his face was comforting. It was as if he was telling me that everything was going to be alright and that I had nothing to fear.

"Boys, go back inside," I heard my wife saying, which disappointed me. Even though she was aware that she shouldn't piss me off, she still did sometimes just so that she could see the look of utter disgust on my face.

What did she think was going to happen now? Did she think I

was going to stay married to her for long? No way. I wasn't going to. If anything, I was already planning on a new life without her.

She spun around and trotted back into the house. In the meantime, I had to plan, and maybe that involved throwing some shit against the fan. I didn't even feel like entertaining the possibility, but maybe there was no other chance.

The serenity of the backyard was unlike any other. It was almost as good as the kitchen, and here I could come to the conclusion that only one thing could be done.

The night was silent, my kids sneaking out of the house and going to play with their new bikes. I could hear their giggles and their jokes, finding it a little sad that they couldn't go out and play with the other kids. It was a shitty thing that they couldn't do that, but in my world, it was either that or risking getting killed or kidnapped.

I didn't feel like thinking about complex matters right now and so I decided to take a break. Take a break? It was something that I didn't do often, I thought. I was so focused on guaranteeing a good future for me and everyone that the thought just never crossed my mind.

"Ready for even more fun than usual?" I asked them when they noticed my presence.

"Daddy! We knew you were going to come," Quinto and Bonifacio said happily in unison, running toward me after leaving their bikes unattended. Seeing that, I had to lift my finger and wag it. They puckered their lips, but still went along with the little reprimand that I was giving.

"Okay, daddy. You always know everything, and we shall never disobey you," Quinto joked, bringing a smile to my face. He was always like that, always cheerful, and I couldn't imagine myself living without him and his brother.

I was going to find out the truth about Orena and then I'd kick their mother out of the house after proving to them that she wasn't the person they thought she was.

That was my promise.

CHAPTER 8

Adamo

I stood behind the door to her apartment, wondering if I was doing the right thing. There was no other way this could be done and I couldn't imagine myself going home tonight. Magda was still there, waiting for me, but I'd already told her that I 'got caught up' in something and she was gullible enough to believe the lie.

The truth was that I kept spending more and more time with Orena, who was the woman of my life and the one I wanted to spend all of my time with. It was for that reason that I brought a beautiful bouquet of red roses with me this time. Someone who didn't know us would look at me and say that I was being corny, but they wouldn't know what was really going on in my mind. It was through acts like these that I won over Magda's heart. If only she hadn't turned into the person she now was, always bitching about something I did. She never was happy with anything I did.

I heard Orena's footsteps nearing the door, thinking back to Silvio and Gildo. They knew that she was now living here and, even though I didn't think that they were going to do anything about it, I was still wary. Gildo was obsessed with her. Silvio also was, but it appeared that his interests in her were due to something else. What that thing was, I didn't know, but I wouldn't put it past him that he was the one who ordered the hit on her. If he was, I'd never forgive him. I'd burn his empire to the ground and he would come out of that wondering what even happened. It just couldn't be, and I would never be able to forgive him.

I groomed myself before coming here. Got a different haircut that I thought made me look sexier. Buffed myself up at the gym, lost a little bit of weight, bought new clothes, did my beard, and sprayed a different perfume on me. All for the purpose of winning Orena's heart over.

I still remembered that first night, when I brought that expensive and special box of chocolates for her. The smile that appeared on her face then… I was always going to remember it, and there was no denying that.

Was I a little nervous? Absolutely, but it wasn't the first time that my pulse was accelerating and my heart was a little tight.

When she was behind the door, I could almost see her eyes through the little peep-hole. I couldn't make them out, but someone with her level of paranoia… I was pretty sure she feared that someone had come here to murder her.

I didn't tell her about this meeting, instead opting to keep her in the dark. Things were going to be different tonight. That night, when we almost kissed, I made a huge mistake. I took it a step too further and it shocked her. She thought that I was taking advantage of her, but that hadn't been the case.

I was just so overjoyed that we were together again and that I could see myself as her new love interest. New? I didn't know about that. If I remembered correctly, she said that she was a virgin when we first met. I didn't know all the details about what happened after that first meeting, our one-night stand, but I was pretty sure – or almost – that she never had someone else in her life.

It was such a pity, especially for someone that was a black queen like her.

She opened the door slowly after figuring out that it was just me. I opened a smile, hoping that it was going to soften her heart. But the seconds passed and I realized that it wasn't going to be so easy, especially because she was still wary about my intentions.

Whenever I was with her, I always made sure that I didn't have my engagement ring. I didn't want her to find out that I was engaged to my fiancée. If she did, I was pretty sure she would never give me a chance. Orena was like that. She was humble, moralistic, and always willing to do the right thing. The threesome was nothing more than a drop in the ocean that composed the morals of her life.

"Hi…" She said, her eyes going up and down, probably realizing that something was at play here. But her eyes then landed on my bouquet and she figured out what was going on here, or at least a part of it. "I didn't expect you to be here tonight."

I widened my smile slightly. "I know, right? I also didn't think that I was going to come, but then I realized that I wanted to be here. I wanted to see you one more time."

"Really?" She asked, wondering if she shouldn't just shut the door in my face, even though she knew she couldn't. I was the one paying for everything. I wasn't going to use that against her, but the thought was in her mind and she couldn't shake it off. "You're so nice."

A moment of nothingness hung in the air. We both didn't know what to say.

"Well, come in, then." And after she finished saying that, I stepped into her apartment room, finding myself in the familiarity of it. I had come here so many times already, spent so many hours in it that it was homier than my own house. "And let me take this bouquet."

She picked it out of my hand, putting it in a small jar with water. I watched her as she did that, watched every movement she performed, paying attention to the way her body moved. I knew I was just overthinking it, but everything that she did was truly special. It was as if time moved in slow motion for me, which was different from anything that ever happened in my life before. Even different from when I fell in love with Magda.

She turned around, asking, "Well, now that you're here, do you mind saying why?"

I cleared my throat, realizing that the sweat that was coming out of my pores was cold. Shit. It was the first time in my life that I was sweating coldly. Orena really was something else, always so sweet and attentive. She always asked me several questions about my life, although she was always mindful not to ask me anything regarding my love life.

"It's about that time when we almost kissed."

"Oh... I didn't think you still remembered that. I mean, we met up so many times since then and the topic never came up. You were always so busy with other things."

"I just want to say that I didn't want you to feel that I was taking advantage of you. That's not what happened. It wasn't my intention."

"That's not what I thought of it, anyway. It took me by surprise, but then I just brushed it off."

"No, I mean it. I was a jerk, thinking that you were already falling in love with me or something like that." She widened her eyes, staring right into my pupils. "And I want to say that... I am in love with you. I don't know how it happened, why it did, but the truth is that it's the way I feel about you."

She didn't know what to say, shifting her weight. Seconds later, when I thought she was going to keep her lips sealed, she replied, "I don't even know what to say," which was funny. She pondered her answer this whole time only to think and say that she was at a loss for words.

"You don't need to say anything. Just do whatever it is that your heart feels and I'll be okay with it."

She took a step toward me, putting her hand on my cheek. "You are a good man. Even when other people say that you aren't, I know you are. You've always shown that you care about me, that you only want what's best for me, and that's more than what most people ever showed to me."

Now, with what she was saying, it was difficult not to feel even more nervous than before. With my heart in my throat, I just realized that she was close to me – closer than she had ever been – and that this was possibly the moment I'd always been waiting for. I felt like I was a teenager all over again, which was certainly messing with my thoughts.

But if there was someone in control of this moment, who was about to kiss her, that person was me. I was the one last inside of her, but I was the first to truly claim her and I wasn't willing to share.

Our lips connected and I pushed her against the wall, pinning her against it, but without hurting her. If I hurt someone pregnant, probably even with my baby, then I wouldn't be able to forgive myself. I would never be able to do that.

When she pulled her head back, I noticed she was breathless. "So, how was that for a first kiss?" I asked, studying her eyes to figure out what she was thinking. It wasn't as if I was a mind reader, but I could pick up on some hints. She enjoyed it, didn't she?

"It was amazing. This whole time, I didn't know what I was missing," she purred, kissing me right back and giggling the whole way through. She was content, more so than she had been in a long time, and it was as though she could even start living a normal life. I wouldn't say that she was, but she thought that she was, and that was almost good enough.

Everything happened so quickly I didn't realize I was already in her bedroom. It was familiar, but not quite so. Even though I had spent so many hours in her apartment, I spent little time in her bedroom, as it was supposed to be. It wasn't like she invited me into the place, after all.

She started to unbutton the buttons of my shirt, widening her smile. One button after the other, she revealed what it hit underneath. My chest. I didn't like boasting about it, especially because I didn't want to come across as someone with a big ego, but I worked out and, these past few months, I spent even more time at the gym.

She traced the outline of my chest with her fingers, enjoying every part of it.

One thing about having sex with a pregnant woman was that I needed to be more careful, but it wasn't cumbersome.

Loving every part of what I was seeing, I wasted no time before sneaking my fingers under her PJ's shirt, pulling it up while feeling the skin of her pregnant belly. This time, it wasn't just about sex, but about the love that I felt for her, and I could tell that she thought the same.

With her shirt out of the way, her breasts were almost exposed. The only thing standing in my way right now was her bra, and I quickly got rid of it after dealing with the hook.

I didn't let it fall to the floor, instead depositing it on her bed, where we were going to do unspeakable things. I grabbed one of her boobs, eliciting a moan out of her mouth. She locked her eyes with me, falling down on the bed and grabbing my tie, which she promptly yanked off.

It seemed I just stole her heart and she could do nothing about it.

CHAPTER 9

Orena

I didn't think I was going to find myself with Adamo tonight, opening myself up for him. But the truth was that no one else had been so caring with me this whole time, making sure that nothing unfavorable happened to me. Whenever I thought of someone I wanted to be with, he was always present.

He dipped his head, pursing his lips as he kissed my engorged and grown belly. That was his way of telling me that it didn't matter who the true father of the baby was, he was going to take care of it.

One thing I was curious about – he didn't have anyone in his life other than me? No girlfriends or someone already hitting on him? It would be a dream if that were the case, but I didn't think much of it.

The man who called me said that he was already with someone else, but I didn't trust him.

I was burning hot, throwing my legs around him and feeling his muscles flexing. He kicked off his pants right away, but didn't do anything about his dark pair of boxer briefs. It looked exquisite on him, making me press one of my fingers against my lips.

I wanted all of this man, but it seemed he was thinking that he should be a tease.

His lips were right in front of my mouth, and I couldn't help myself, kissing him then and there, showing him that nothing could stand in my way. His lips were soft, sweet, and delicious. I could never have enough of them, and I was pretty sure that he thought the same way regarding my lips.

He pulled his head back, murmuring, "I don't even know what I should be saying right now."

"How about nothing, cowboy?" I purred, hinting at the fact that he liked riding on horseback for leisure.

"Good enough for me," he replied, kissing my cheek and then moving down the side of my neck, going all the way where my breasts were. I thought that Adamo was going to land his lips there too, but he stopped. My eyes met his one more time, and I couldn't help but wonder what was going on in his mind right now.

"It's not going to be so easy," he joked, settling his hand on my belly and gliding it up. I felt it traversing across my skin, stopping when he was no more than mere inches from encountering the lower part of my boob.

"This is so unfair," I muttered, tilting my head backward and moaning when he moved his hand just slightly further up. He was going to trace my breast with it, and I didn't know if I could resist the surge of pleasure that was going to flare up in my entire body.

"No, it's not. You're getting everything you deserve," he replied, pecking at my lips. It was nothing more than a short kiss and it didn't last more than a second, but it was already making me miss it.

"You are destroying me," I crooned, thinking that I was going to find the part of him where he felt some mercy for me, but finding nothing, I realized moments later.

So much so that he wasted no time before sliding his hand slightly further up, cupping my breast. When his fingers were pressing against it, it was as if time moved in slow motion for me. His skin was a little rough, but nothing that was going to get in the way of my enjoyment. After all, it wasn't the first time that I felt his skin.

"Gosh, you are so delicious. You are so perfect. How is it possible that someone like you was a virgin the entire time before that night?" He asked, but I didn't entertain the possibility of answering him. After all, there was no need to answer the man.

"I'm not even going to say anything about that," I murmured, trying to turn around slowly, but soon realizing that his body was pinning me against the bed. He was everywhere around me and I felt so tiny, even with my engorged belly.

His abs were pressed against it, reminding me that this wasn't a dream. No. This was truly happening and I was giving myself for the man that always took care of me.

"Then, don't say anything else."

That's what he said, but I was pretty sure that he didn't mean it. At the end of the day, he loved my voice too much for that.

His fingers moved again, finding my nipple. When he pressed them against it, pinching it, I felt a surge of pleasure flaring up in my body. It was everywhere, contaminating every part of it.

I planted my hands on his back, digging my fingers into his skin.

"Stop," I pleaded, not knowing if that was going to be enough.

A moment of silence, with nothing happening, and I could finally breathe again.

"Why?" He asked, the following thought probably popping up in his mind: he wanted to breach me. He wanted to go inside of me again, and it was difficult for me not to do that. I was going to allow him to.

"I almost couldn't breathe anymore. Having sex is so difficult when you're pregnant."

And it wasn't just pregnant, but I was probably in my ninth month already.

He groaned slightly, moving down so that he kissed my belly. He looked up, finding my lazy eyes.

"You have nothing to fear. I'm going to be here for the baby and

I don't even care whose baby it is."

Now that I remembered it, I didn't have triplets. It was just one baby, which meant that it belonged to just one of the men that had me that night.

"I know, but it was still so difficult."

"Then, I'm going to go slower," he promised, moving up so that he kissed me again, making sure that it lasted no more than a couple seconds, which wasn't enough.

"Thank you…"

The thanks were unnecessary, but I still felt that it was fitting. The man wasted no time, moving down slowly as he peppered my skin with several kisses, making sure that they were slow and almost everlasting. He was like that. He liked to take his time.

"You're such a jerk," I murmured, feeling as if every word punctured my heart.

"Well, you like the way I am," he said and it was no lie.

I glided my hands down his back, cherishing the muscles, how firm they were and how they flexed under my touch. I continued making my way to the lower part of his back, searching for his ass. I wanted to touch it, to feel what it was like, and he did nothing to stop me.

Moments later, my fingers finally reached the skin that I was looking for. I cupped each of his asscheeks, moving my fingers around them as I enjoyed how soft they were. And not just that, but also exquisitely smooth.

I reopened my eyes, spotting the tattoo on his chest. It was the tattoo of an eagle, which made me wonder what the history behind it was. I had no idea if he would ever enlighten me about that, but the thought was in my mind nonetheless. Perhaps it was something for another time.

"You are naughtier than you want most people to think you are," he said and it wasn't a lie. I had always been naughty.

"I never said I wasn't," I argued, turning around slowly and finding out that, this time, Adamo let me do that.

I was now with my back facing him, feeling his eyes going up and down, taking in every inch of my body. Moments later, I heard him pushing down his pair of boxer briefs. I wished I could peek over my shoulder to see what his cock was like in person again, but I couldn't. It was already taking me so much effort to even be on my knees on the bed, with my ass raised so that Adamo could do whatever he wanted.

"I could almost regret what I'm doing," I confessed, biting my bottom lip when I felt his fingers tracing the curvature of my ass. He was doing that excessively slowly. Then, he gripped his cock, stroking it. He was getting it ready. He was going to penetrate me, and I could already imagine how I was going to feel when he was inside of me.

"You aren't regretting anything," he affirmed as he parted my asscheeks, lowering his body until his head was between my legs. I could feel his nose breathing against it, feeling my smell. I wished he had told me he was going to come so that I had taken a shower and better prepared myself for this, but it looked like the lack of those things didn't impede him from enjoying himself.

"You still smell the same," he murmured against my ass, putting his tongue out and then giving it a long, everlasting lick. It was enough to make me arch my back, hoping that he was going to do the same again.

As if Adamo read my mind, he gave it another lick, and then another, and then one more, making sure that the last one was always slower than the one that came before.

Each time that he licked my ass, I felt as if I was going to pass out. My toes curled when he started to rub my clit over and over, his speed dangerously slow. He wasn't doing this for my enjoyment as much as he was doing for my torment.

Sweat was all over my body, pooling on my forehead.

Breathing was as painful as it was before and I didn't think that it was going to get easier.

"I love you so much," Adamo murmured, moving so that he

was even closer against me. I felt his cock brushing against my ass. I didn't hear him going for a package of condom, which meant that he was going to do this without using one. I bit my bottom lip, just imagining what I was going to feel like when his shaft was pounding in and out of me and he became one with me.

As his fingers moved around my shoulders and then down to my waist, he said, "I'm going to be extremely careful with you. You have nothing to worry about."

I knew he told me the truth, but it was still difficult to imagine that he could be careful. Nevertheless, at this point, I already trusted Adamo with my life, and thus I didn't object.

When his hands were pressing into my waist, he pulled me slightly closer to him, his cock nudging the entrance of my tunnel. I held my breath when I felt it breaching the initial barrier, going all the way inside. It wasn't like the first time when he popped my hymen, but it was just as good.

When his cockhead was touching the end of my womb, I closed my eyes tightly and held my breath again. He stretched my walls beyond anything I thought possible, pain flaring up in all parts of my body.

I felt him shifting again, his lips close to my right ear this time.

"How are you feeling right now?" He asked and I could feel that the question was genuine. He truly cared about me and only wanted the best for me.

"Like I'm on the moon," I replied and I knew that he smiled at that.

"Perfect. It means that I can go on," he purred, rolling his hips. His pace was slow in the beginning, but then he picked it up, making sure that he hit all the right spots every time.

Minutes later, I felt his dick throbbing inside of me, shooting rope after rope of come in my tunnel. It was warm and extremely sticky, making me moan and groan. And then I came with him, thinking that I was going to black out.

It didn't happen and I was overjoyed when he turned me

around, depositing me on the bed. His lips came crashing down against mine one more time before he said how much he loved me.

The next few moments were hazy. All I remembered was falling asleep.

CHAPTER 10

Orena

I remembered waking up and finding out that I wasn't in the same room. Rather, I was in a dark, unforgiving place. I couldn't move my body, finding out that I was strapped to a chair. I scanned the surroundings, even though using my eyes was tough and painful. I never felt so much pain before.

No more than a couple of hours ago I was in my room, making love with the best man of my life, and now here I was. What the hell happened, and what was even happening?

I couldn't believe that someone managed to kidnap me. I mean, that couldn't have been the case, right? The apartment building where I lived was protected by dozens of guards, and they were all Adamo's most trusted men.

Unless one or some of them betrayed him... I didn't know what happened, but I was pretty sure that, by now, he had to be looking into all the possibilities and searching for me, too.

I remembered those men that tried killing me. Could it be them this time, too? If it were them, then I didn't think I had much more time. They were going to realize that I'd already woken up, ask whatever questions they had for me, and then take me out of this world. I wouldn't even have enough time to remember all the good things that happened in my life.

I was weak, but tried swinging my body left and right anyway, eventually toppling over. Strapped to the chair, my arms roped behind the back support, I knew that what I did was utterly pointless. I wasn't thinking straight. That much was clear.

Dust billowed up when I breathed heavily through my mouth. I thought that I heard someone coming this way, but then I realized that it was just my mind playing tricks on me again. It was a rat, scurrying away when it realized that I was looking at it.

But then, a shadowy figure popped up behind the slightly open door, glaring at me with mean eyes. I couldn't make out who it was and it wouldn't be different if the lighting was better.

All I could see was darkness, white light, and his crimson eyes glaring at me. It was as if he was thinking about all the ways he was going to kill me now.

"He was using you this whole time and you were so stupid you didn't even realize that he was," the man lamented and his voice was clear enough. Even though I couldn't make out what he looked like, his voice was sufficient to tell me who he was.

It was Silvio. I had no idea how he managed to capture me, but here I was.

It was him. How could it be anyone else? I thought, realizing that everything made sense. He was the one who put a price on my head, the one who tried to murder me, and I was pretty sure that it was because of the baby.

And I once thought that he was a good man. I once had a crush on him.

"So, are we finally ready to talk?" He asked, stepping toward me. When the light wasn't hitting him from behind, I could finally make out his face. I could finally see that he was suffering right now. I had no idea why, how, or how it was possible that he could even feel anything remotely close to pain, but the truth was that he was.

If there was something I was good at, it was extracting those things when I was in the presence of other people. Sometimes, I could read their minds.

"I don't have anything to say to you. You just kidnapped me. You took me away from the only man that truly cared about me."

"I don't think so. As I said, he was using you and you were too stupid to notice it."

I didn't want to argue with him, but what else was there to do? I couldn't move my body, I was on the floor, it was filthy, and I wanted nothing more than to punch the guy that was in front of me until he was dead.

"You were stupid enough to try freeing yourself, but I'm going to help you again. I'm going to help you up," he said, stepping to me, grabbing me with his hands and then lifting me up, chair included.

When I was seated, he put his hands on my shoulders, staring into my eyes.

"Can we finally talk about what happened?" He asked, making me realize that something just flashed in the corner of my vision. I lowered my eyes to where it happened, noticing a marriage ring on his finger.

"You are… Married?" I asked, not knowing how he was going to take that question. I had no idea he had just recently gotten married. Or maybe he had been this whole time and hid it from me.

He took his hand off my shoulder right away, clenching it. His eyes darted down as they found his marriage ring. For a couple of moments, Silvio said nothing, making me wonder what was going on in his head.

"Yeah, I guess I am."

The way he said that showed me he was hiding something. It was difficult to figure out what it was. In the meantime, the only thing I was worried about, besides escaping this place, was my baby. I hadn't even thought of a name yet for him. I thought I was going to wait until I figured out who the father was, but I didn't think anymore I was going to have enough time for that.

I didn't feel any pain, and then I noticed that my baby was

moving inside my belly. Thank goodness. I thought that he might have been hurt when I was kidnapped.

"Were you still married when…?"

"Does it matter?" He asked, putting his hand back on my shoulder, doing everything in his power to make me feel powerless and small.

"You're going to tell me everything that's happened since that night. Are you somehow trying to use the pregnancy against me?"

I widened my eyes, rebuking his accusation by saying, "I don't even know who the father of the baby is."

He opened his mouth, studying my facial expression. He realized that I told him the truth, didn't he?

"You are lying. I know you are."

"I'm not. Look deeply into my eyes and tell me that I'm lying. If I'm lying, then you can do whatever you want and I'll feel that it's justified."

He didn't say anything, his eyes turning left and right and up and down slowly and carefully. He didn't just study what my eyes were telling him, but also everything that he could perceive in my facial expression. It was unchanged and serious. Silvio knew that I didn't omit the truth.

"Well, we still need to find out who the father of the baby is."

"You said that you feared I was going to use the pregnancy against you. Why? I would never do such a thing. I didn't even know you were married. Are you afraid that your wife is going to find out about it?" I asked, prodding what I thought was one of his weak points.

He turned around slowly as he moved away from me. I was just happy that his breath wasn't against my face anymore. I felt that I could finally breathe again.

"Not because of my wife, but my children. My boys mean the world to me."

I felt a pang of guilt, realizing that I was feeling hatred toward him this whole time without considering that he had a life outside of here. He had a life outside of the mafia world. He was a human being like everyone else.

"I didn't know you had a family."

"Yeah, whatever."

After a moment of silence, he added, "I'm going to get your saliva. I need to run a DNA test to make sure the baby isn't mine. It was my fault what happened that night."

He approached me, but I struggled, making the chair fall over again. I felt my body falling heavily on the floor, pain surging up in my body.

"What a mess you just made again. You can't even behave like a normal person," he grumbled, pulling me up slowly so that the chair was in the position where it was supposed to be. This time, I noticed he was gentler when doing that, which was certainly something I didn't expect from him.

I guess he finally saw that I never planned on using the pregnancy against him.

Nevertheless, there was something I was curious about him, which I wanted to ask right now.

"You said that you don't mind if your wife finds out about my pregnancy. Why is that?"

He shook his head, swiping the swab inside my mouth and collecting some saliva. It was quick and painless, almost like it didn't happen. But now he had my DNA with him and I couldn't shake that off.

"I don't think that's something you need to know."

"If all you needed was my saliva, then why did you kidnap me?" I asked, studying his eyes and realizing that, if it was possible, he wouldn't be doing this right now.

"I just wanted to ask you some questions. I wanted to be with you face-to-face."

"And what are you planning on doing, now that you have what you need?"

"I'm certainly not going to give you back to Adamo."

My heart raced. Being again with him was everything I wanted right now. I wanted to be in his warm arms, with him telling me that everything was going to be fine.

"Then, what? Are you going to keep me as your prisoner for the rest of my life?"

He walked away, stopping behind the doorway.

"Until I figure out what to do with you. I'm not so sure I want to do anything with you right now. I need time to think, time to reflect on everything that happened."

He took a step toward the hallway and I stopped him when I asked, "You aren't happy with your wife, right? What did she do?"

He turned his head so that he was looking at me over his shoulder. "You're oddly curious about things you don't have to know anything about. Why?"

"Are you going to answer my question?" I asked, hoping that he was, but I didn't have high hopes.

"No…" He answered, closing the door and leaving me where I was. I didn't have any reasons to feel anything other than absolute hatred for the man, but I finally realized that he was a human being just like I was. He was trudging through a lot of things in his personal life, things that he wanted to keep hidden from me.

CHAPTER 11

Orena

"You're going to be living here for the time being," Silvio announced, pulling up the sack on my head. I examined the surroundings, finding out that I was in an extremely luxurious and well-decorated room. It was like the room that my dollhouse had.

I looked to the left, finding the bed and I wanted to lie down on it right now. The covers, the bedsheets, the pillows, and pretty much everything else that made it what it was looked so perfect and comfortable. It was much better than the bed I had in Adamo's apartment, which wasn't something I thought I'd ever say.

He was behind me, his guards with him. He didn't think that I was going to do anything stupid, but he couldn't take any chances, regardless.

I then looked to the right, finding the closet. I opened it when he said, "It already has everything you're going to need."

"So, you're keeping me as your prisoner, but at least the place is good," I said, trying to smile, but feeling like I couldn't. After all, why was I going to smile at the man that kidnapped me and was now keeping me as his prisoner?

Adamo was different. He loved me and didn't put me in a place like this. Checking the outside for a moment, I could tell that we were far away from any civilization. Trees surrounded the property, a huge and impenetrable wall around it too.

Guards were posted everywhere. Even if I tried escaping from this place, I didn't think that I'd go anywhere, not to mention that I couldn't see any freeways and cars driving on them. I'd have no one to help me, and I was pretty sure that that was one of the reasons why he picked this place.

"It's much different than what Adamo did to you. He wasn't just keeping you as his prisoner, but as his pet. He made you think that you fell in love with him, didn't he?" He asked, approaching me and signaling with his head for his men to leave.

I guess that he realized there was no chance I was going to attack him right now.

"You don't know how kind he can be, how sweet he is," I said, closing the closet after finding a huge, complete collection of clothing pieces that I could wear. Dresses, shirts, pants, high-heels, and pretty much everything else one could think of. I was living in a mansion. I didn't see the outside when I was brought here, but I knew it was. The outside of the property was telling enough, especially with all the open space, the multiple vehicles positioned in different spots, and all the other buildings that I found with my eyes, including what appeared to be a small chapel.

Was Silvio planning on getting married again here? Was this his retreat? Was he planning on marrying someone else?

"I know the kind of person he is. Much more than you do. Did you know that he's engaged to his fiancée and thinking about dumping her? Do you think that, with you, things will be different?" He asked, approaching me and making me moonwalk toward the wall.

I felt my ass bumping against it, realizing that he was cornering me again. I should be fighting against him, but it was difficult to do so when he was just so much stronger than me. Not to mention that I was pregnant and I could do nothing that could harm the baby.

What he told me shocked me. "No, I didn't know anything

about that."

I knew Adamo was with someone else, but I thought that they weren't that deep in their relationship. I didn't think he was considering wedding her.

His eyes softened up. "See? I told you that he was lying this whole time."

Adamo really did omit the truth, which was a blow to our relationship, but it was still not enough to shatter it. I wasn't going to start hating Adamo without giving him the benefit of telling me his side of the story. If he was engaged to his fiancée, then why did he fall in love with me? Didn't he feel bad for her?

Silvio being so close to me now didn't help, either. He was still so sexy, especially when he was so dominating. He put one of his hands on my shoulder, caressing it.

Why was he doing that? He wasn't going to suddenly tell me that he fell in love with me as well, right?

I didn't think so. Whatever he was feeling right now for me, it was nothing more than a carnal urge.

His hand was big, heavy, and calloused. I wanted to touch it, but I needed not to do anything that might tell him I still had a slight crush on him.

"I'm not going to condemn Adamo without first talking to him, and I demand that you let me out of this house so that I can do that. I am in love with him. If you think that that's going to change, think again. Our love is strong and unbreakable."

He smiled mildly.

"You're so cute when you're pissed."

I didn't say anything, feeling that it wasn't worth it.

"So, you're going to keep me here forever?"

"I'm going to keep you here, where you should be living, for as long as possible. After all, Adamo wants you back and he will do anything for you."

"So, you're just going to blackmail him?" I asked, trying to push him away from me, but realizing that he wasn't going to budge. He stayed where he was, his body inches from touching mine. I felt waves of heat rising up in my body, making me squirm my legs.

"I'm going to talk to him, in person, and I'll make some demands. I hope he understands them. Otherwise, you'll never leave this place."

I narrowed my eyes slightly. "If you're so determined on doing that, then what about your children? What about your boys? Do you think that they would forgive you if they found out that you are keeping me as your prisoner?"

I knew that I was crossing a line, but he still needed to hear that. Silvio was spoiled, just like everyone that controlled a mafia family. He thought that everyone sucked up to him, that everyone wanted to be on his good side.

I feared he was going to hit me, but then he did something else.

CHAPTER 12

Silvio

Orena's audacity was impressive. Even when she was pinned against the wall, pregnant, on the verge of giving birth, and had no strength to fight against me, she still dared say the things she just did. The question she asked… It was always going to remain in my mind.

But at least, if she was going to be an asshole to me, then I could at least take a little advantage of this moment.

Thinking that, I cupped her cheeks, connected our lips, and waited to see if she was going to fight back. If she did, if she pushed me back with all of her strength, then I wouldn't continue. I wouldn't insist.

But the seconds passed and she actually melted in my embrace. I hated her, but I still wanted to kiss her, and I could tell that she thought the same way.

Our lips rubbed against each other, brushing up and down and left and right, becoming much more than just a kiss. Her lips were wet, extremely warm, and her big belly was against my abs.

She couldn't do anything, not even move her arms. She was paralyzed where she was, still trying to figure out what was happening.

Orena never suspected that I was just going to kiss her like this, right?

I pulled my head back when I noticed that she was having difficulty breathing. She was breathless, studying my eyes. I could almost read what she was thinking.

"What the hell was that?" She asked, huffing.

"I just wanted a little taste, a memory of what happened that night."

"You really don't feel bad for your wife and you wanted to diss Adamo for doing the same."

"Because of that, but also because he lied. Didn't I tell you that he never told you he was engaged?"

"Then, what's the difference when compared to you?" Orena asked, narrowing her eyes slightly. She looked determined. I figured that it didn't matter what happened now, she wasn't going to lose her sassiness and bravery. She was going to keep fighting against me.

"I was upfront when you asked me about it."

"And I don't think I ever asked if he had someone else. I just assumed that he was single, just like I thought you were."

"But it was different. He has an engagement ring. He hid it from you so that you felt more comfortable around him."

Orena opened her mouth, but closed it right after. She realized that I was right. I had no problems telling my partners that I was looking for someone else. Adamo, on the other hand, wanted to keep everything under wraps.

"Can you still really trust him after everything he did? After all the lies?" I asked, examining her expression and her eyes to figure out what she was thinking.

It was almost there. She was almost starting to believe it, that Adamo was nothing more than an asshole.

I placed my hand on her waist, feeling the softness of her skin. Now that I realized the DNA test was going to confirm my suspicion, I couldn't help but think that my hatred for her was now unfounded. When I assumed that she was hiding the pregnancy to use it against me, to make my boys hate me, I loathed her, but now things were different. I realized that I'd been wrong.

"Should I even answer that?" Orena asked, doing nothing more than keeping her hands against my chest. She wasn't trying to push me away with all of her strength, though. It was as if she was telling me that she was enjoying this, even though I was her captor.

"You can do whatever you want. You know that, in here, you are more than my prisoner."

"For some reason, I don't quite believe that."

After a moment of silence, I asked, "Did you like it?"

She widened her eyes tightly, breathing slowly. "Like what?"

"The kiss. You didn't fight back strongly, which means there's something about it you aren't telling me." I smiled devilishly, though not too broadly. It was just enough so that she could see the perfection of my lips.

"I'm not even going to say anything about that. It's not worth it," she hissed, moving her hands around my body, feeling the curves of my chest. She loved it, didn't she? At the end of the day, Orena was like any other woman, always wanting to be with a strong man.

"Maybe you should," I purred, lowering my head and inhaling her smell. It was natural, perfect, and I wanted to smell it for hours on end. It was a pity that I couldn't.

"What the hell are you doing?" She asked, trying to push me away from her, but it didn't work. I had Orena cornered and she loved that, didn't she?

I pulled my head back slightly, gazing into her eyes. I hated this woman until no more than a couple of hours ago. Why the hell was I acting like this right now? It was as if an external force was controlling me.

"If you don't want me to continue, you can just ask me to stop," I offered, but I didn't know if she was going to accept it.

She bit her bottom lip, stepping away from me suddenly. "I'm not going to do anything with you. You're keeping me here to take advantage of me."

As I said, I wasn't going to force myself on her. If she didn't want me to kiss her and do things beyond that, then I wasn't going to. I wasn't a rapist, after all.

"I wanted to kiss you, but I won't do anything beyond that. Not after you just showed me that you aren't comfortable with it."

"How chivalrous of you. You really want to come off as a good guy, but you aren't."

I stepped toward her, but she walked away from me.

A moment of silence ensued and I wondered if she was going to say anything else.

"You are free to walk around the property, but you can't leave. If any of the guys hit on you, you need to tell me everything. I'm going to keep you protected, even from my men."

I presumed she was going to say something, but then I realized that she was crying. The twinkle of a light rolling down her cheek and a sob… She really was crying, which wasn't something I foresaw. I thought she was incapable of feeling such a thing. She was always so strong and brave, after all.

I approached her, sitting down with her on the bed. The mattress sagged under our weight, her body seeming unbelievably tiny right now. I had an arm around her shoulders to show that she had my support now, no matter what.

After a couple more sobs and tears, she said, "I shouldn't be crying. Not with you around."

"Why not?" I asked, realizing now that I cared about her, even though it was something I hid this whole time. I hid it from her, from me, and I didn't think it was going to come out now.

"You smell other peoples' weaknesses and use them as weapons. That's who you are. You are a terrible person – a monster."

"You're not going to get anywhere by insulting me. You have the option of telling me about what's going on in your mind right now, and you can either do that or pretend that this isn't happening. If you choose the latter, I'll respect your choice."

Moments later, she didn't say anything else, making me wonder what was even going on in her mind. Again, I couldn't help but feel that I was betraying my initial feelings for her.

"You're making me realize that I should never have let it happen. I shouldn't have fallen in love with him," she stammered, the words coming out of her mouth quickly despite that.

I didn't suspect that she was thinking that, but now that I realized that was the case, I couldn't help but feel that it was a win. If she was pissed with Adamo about his lie, then all was good. I mean, not 'all' was good, but it was better than before.

"You're hurt because of the lies he kept from you this whole time, aren't you?"

"I suppose I should be thinking that you're lying too, but now it all makes sense. He was taking advantage of me too and keeping the truth hidden."

"Well, this has worked a little faster than I thought it was going to," I commented, not knowing how she was going to take that.

She perked up one of her eyebrows. "What do you mean? You're not doing the same thing he did to me, right?" She asked. I could see how curious she was, already forgetting – or at least, pushing aside – all the bad things I did to her.

"No, it's nothing like that. I would never do such a thing to you. You know what I'm like. I prefer being upfront about what I'm feeling. I would never hide such a thing from you."

"No, I suppose you would never, not that I think you are someone more respectable. At the end of the day, you are criminal like he is," Orena said, wiping one of her tears. She sobbed one more time, but stood up and went over to the window anyway.

I waited to see if she was going to say anything, and then she said, "I knew I shouldn't have fallen in love. It was never good for me, and now you opened my eyes to that."

"It wasn't my intention. I didn't want to break the strong and healthy relationship you had with him."

I couldn't help but rake her body from bottom to top, loving the way she was just standing there behind the window. I wanted to thread her hair with my fingers, to move them through it, and love her skin and feel how smooth it was again. Nevertheless, if something like that was to happen, I needed to win her heart over first. It would be difficult, considering that she loathed me until not too long ago, after all.

When she turned around, I noticed how her breasts jiggled gently, showing me just how well-endowed she was. The first thought that popped up in my mind was how much I wanted to feel the weight of her boobs with my hands, but doing so was impossible at the moment.

Nevertheless, she wasn't shy. Orena never was. The cleavage on her chest told me as much. It was perfect, extremely round, and showing more of her skin than it should. It was as if she was using that to her advantage, which I wouldn't put past her.

Her lips parted slightly, showing me just how crimson, big, succulent, and heavy they seemed. I imagined her widening them a little more, wrapping them around my cock, and then moving up and down along it. She would seize my balls with her hands, giving them a little squeeze. She would wet my cockhead, swirling her tongue around it.

Nevertheless, those things were for another time and I wasn't going to kindle false hope.

I went to the door and said, "I'm going now, but I can be back anytime. When I come here, it will be a surprise."

Orena didn't say anything, opting to remain where she was. Before I was out of sight, I took one last look at her, loving the shape of her legs. What I wouldn't do right now to slide my fingers up and down along them, feeling the smoothness and softness of her skin. She would plant her hands on my shoulders and would cry out my name.

Gosh, why was I so horny?

CHAPTER 13

Adamo

I didn't know what happened. One moment Orena was by my side on the bed, sleeping with me. One moment I was spooning her and then the next she was gone. I could still feel the warmth of her body against mine. She made me feel like I wasn't a monster. She made me feel that I deserved her, which was a lot more than I could say about my fiancée.

Whatever transpired, I had a traitor in my family. Whoever he was, he was going to suffer the consequences of his crime.

I sat up, got off the bed, put my clothes on, and called Espedito. He picked up the call right away, saying, "Boss?"

"It's me. We have a traitor, and I want to find out what happened to the girl that was in room 301. She was with me. She's someone special to me and just disappeared. I had dozens of men posted around the property. They should've been keeping an eye on her."

"What was her name?"

I gave him her full name, hoping that he was going to sniff her out, wherever she was.

Moments later, he said, "Give me whatever else you have on her and I'll see what I can dig out."

"Just make sure that you find her."

"I'm going to, boss. You have my word on that."

I ended the call, pacing around in the room. It was difficult to think about what I should do right now. Given what I knew, what she said about what happened to her before we met again, it was possible that the same people who tried to kill her then kidnapped her now.

I clenched my hand, fearing that they were hurting her right now.

Then, a thought popped up in my mind. It had to be one of them who did it. Either Gildo or Silvio, and I disliked those possibilities. I didn't want to go up against them, especially not when I was busy with other things, but it was also true that I didn't have another choice.

Just when I thought I was going to have to do something stupid, my phone started to ring. I pulled it up, reading what the screen showed. I thought that I was going to find out that it was nothing more than a robocaller trying to scam me, but that didn't appear to be the case.

It was anything but that. Espedito. He'd come to tell me that he just figured out what happened, and I was desperate for the truth. So much so that when I put my phone next to my ear, it hurt me. I slammed it against my head.

"Espedito, tell me everything you know. That was quick, so I'm hoping you haven't called me empty-handed."

"I have, but I'm not sure you are going to like the answer."

The seconds passed and he explained everything, including that it was none other than my own men who betrayed me. I looked at that without knowing what I should do right now. Silvio penetrated my mafia family. He found a way in, played me for a fool, and took advantage of that information to kidnap the one person that meant the most to me.

I didn't know what he thought he was doing. I was aware that he knew she was with me, but I didn't think he was going to dare.

I needed to call him. It was the only thing that could be done right now.

In light of that, I fished my phone out, punching several numbers. The line called him for what felt like minutes, and then he picked it up. For the first few seconds, I thought that he wasn't going to say anything, but then he did.

"Adamo, it's so good to know that it's you who's calling me right now. I thought that it was someone else. But it's your number and it really is you. You're braver than I thought."

"Stop joking and pretending that you don't know what's happening."

"And what is happening?"

"You kidnapped Orena, didn't you? I don't know how you pulled that off, especially when I was still sleeping with her, but I'm going to get her back, no matter the cost."

"What?" He asked, trying to sound surprised, but it wasn't going to work. Did he think that I was stupid or something like that? Espedito was my most trusted advisor. His words meant the world to me, and I knew he was right when he said that Silvio had Orena.

"I could go to war over what you did, and I don't think that's something you want right now," I growled, fisting my hand. I wished I could tear open his neck right now, and it was such a pity that I couldn't.

"You're being delusional right now. I know who Orena is, but if you really lost her, then that's on you and not on me. I'd never do something like that. I have my principles," he replied, sounding condescending. His condescending tone made my blood boil. If he was right in front of me now, in the same room, I wouldn't hesitate before destroying his life little by little.

"So, what do you think is going to happen now? I know you're lying. You're going to give Orena back to me and then we'll pretend that nothing happened, though this is the only time that I'm doing this. I'm not usually so kind."

After a moment of silence, he answered, "Look, there's something that you need to know and I don't think that you're going to like it."

"Finally ready to tell me that you were just bullshitting me right now?"

"Ahhh, fine. Yeah. She's here, but you aren't allowed to see her. You should be more focused on your fiancée and making sure that you'll have a great marriage with her. I mean, did you think that you were going to be able to keep both of them or something like that?"

I clenched my teeth. I had no idea what he was implying, but I didn't like any of it, anyway.

"What the hell are you saying?" I hissed. If he kept this up, I would have no choice but to start a war against him.

"You know exactly what I'm saying. You know what you did before. You are trying to keep both your fiancée and Orena for yourself, aren't you, you motherfucker?" He growled, making me feel that something else was going on here. Whatever that was, though, I wanted to find out the truth.

"What?"

"Orena told me everything, how you're trying to woo her. She even fell in love with you. I was conflicted before I decided to take her away from you, but now I realize that I made the right choice. You hurt her."

"What the hell are you even implying right now?" I asked, already stepping outside and sitting in my limo. I waved my hand at the driver, urging him to drive me to my house. It was where my HQ was and where I was going to prepare what I was going to do. I had no idea if I was going to truly start a war, but I didn't have another choice. Silvio was the only one who could decide what I should do right now.

"Look, whatever you're trying to do right now, it's not going to work. You can come here. I'm not in America, so get ready to take a plane to Germany. I'll give you the address and then you'll be able to talk to her in person. She'll tell you everything."

I drummed my fingers on my right thigh, pondering his

words.

I had no idea what Silvio had planned, but it couldn't be anything good. I mean, he was willing to let me see Orena face-to-face without putting up any resistance between us? Just like that?

If that was the case, then I was okay with it. The only problem was that I didn't trust his words at all.

I put my phone against my chest, saying to the driver, "Take me to the airport and buy a ticket to Germany. We're going there."

He looked at me with a shocked expression on his face, but then he lowered his eyebrows. He knew that something huge was brewing, but also that he couldn't do anything about it.

Still drumming my fingers on my thigh, I said, "I hope you aren't trying to pull a fast one on me. If that's the case, you'll be surprised at what I can do when I'm pissed."

"I promise that's not the case."

I took a deep breath in, looking outside and realizing that I was probably not going to be seeing that view in a long time. I had no idea how much time I was going to spend in Germany, but it was probably going to be a significant amount of it.

"And I hope you didn't hurt her. I'll never forgive you if you did."

"I would never do something like that," he hissed, showing me that he was being serious about that.

With him saying that, the next thing I did was end the call and put my phone against my thigh. I looked outside again, admiring the view for what felt like an eternity. I had an opportunity to be with my loved one again, wondering how the hell Silvio still managed to sneak one of his soldiers into my family. I was going to have to confront him about that.

I took a plane to Germany about an hour after that, finding myself in their territory. Silvio didn't lie when he said that he was going to give me an address. Nevertheless, I didn't know if it was the right one. All I knew was that I was going there, to what appeared to be the middle of nowhere, where all I could see were hills, trees, and cottages.

If my queen was living there, then I wondered what she was thinking right now. Did she miss me? I didn't know, but the question was pertinent. It was one of the things I most wanted to ask her when I met up with her again.

The driver entered what appeared to be a huge, impressive estate, pulling over by the front of the mansion. I opened the door without waiting for the driver to open it for me. Jumping outside, I waited to see if Orena was already coming, but I didn't hear anything from the other side of the door.

It was a huge, impressive door that stood out, but it didn't appear that anything was happening behind it. I wanted to bust into the house, break the door down, but I couldn't. For now, I was going to play along with what Silvio wanted me to do. He wanted me here and that was fine. He couldn't kill me, anyway. Not without starting a war that he didn't want.

Minutes later, the door opened and he stepped outside. I clenched my hand, doing everything in my power not to attack him right now. As far as I was concerned, he was the one who kidnapped my loved one, and that was something that just could never be forgiven.

And he looked pretty confident about how this was going to turn out too, I noticed. The smile on his face didn't lie about that. It was more like a smirk. The smirk of someone who thought he had everything under control.

"Where's Orena?" I hissed, taking a step toward him. Everyone around us looked tense, their jaws clenched and tight. Every time two Mafia bosses met up, nothing good came out. That was something they always remembered whenever it happened.

"First tell me what your intentions with her are," he demanded, pulling up the side of his shirt and showing that he had a gun with him. I couldn't help but let out a snicker. Did he think that something like that was going to intimidate me? It was nothing more than a ruse.

And I planned on seeing through to the end of it.

CHAPTER 14

Gildo

The front gate opened, the limousine moving through the opening and then pulling over. I knew that I was going to find both of them there, but it was still a surprise seeing that we were all going to be together again. And it wasn't even for a normal business meeting like all the tower times.

Oh no. This was for something else. I should have put Orena at the back of my head a long time ago, but the truth was that I wasn't able to. Something about her kept calling me back to her, to being with her, and I knew that I felt something strong for her. It was difficult to put my finger on it, but if I had to guess, it probably had something to do with the fact that she was pregnant.

Could the baby be mine? I didn't know, but Silvio said that he ran the DNA tests. I had no idea if that meant he wasn't the father, but all things considered, he had to know something that I didn't.

The driver opened the door of the car and I wasn't surprised when Adamo glared at me. The only thing going on in his mind right now was how much he wanted to kill me. He wanted to turn me into a pulp of meat. If only he could do that without ramifications, I was pretty sure he would. The only problem was that he couldn't. Not without turning Germany into a warzone.

"Nice to see you guys again," I lied, getting nothing more than mean stares at me.

"I think that we can finally discuss what happened," Silvio suggested, lifting his hands slightly. What the hell was he even thinking he was doing right now? Did he think that he was going to be the voice of reason among us or something like that?

"What are you trying to say?" Adamo asked, looking ready to lunge at his enemy and tear his neck open. His hands were clenched. The only thing standing between him and igniting a war right now was his self-control. He didn't look it, but he was a composed and cold guy when he needed to. And right now, he needed those things more than anything else.

"I'm saying that Orena's already going into labor. We have everything she's going to need to deliver the baby here. Unfortunately, I don't have your DNAs, so I wasn't able to tell whose baby he is, but I'm pretty sure that at least it isn't mine, which gives me conflicted feelings about it, I have to admit."

"Conflicted feelings about it?" I asked, stepping toward them, but keeping my distance.

"I was hoping that it was mine so that I could have a strong and confident claim on Orena… but the truth is that, after living for so long with my wife, I want someone else. And I think that someone else is Orena. She's perfect in every way I could think and she plays with my feelings more than anyone else ever did."

"What?" Adamo growled, his eyes growing redder. The hatred that he felt toward Silvio was nothing short of indescribable. I could almost feel it pulsing out of him. "I don't trust a word of what you're saying."

"Whether you trust me or not right now is insignificant. I can show you that she's in the operation room and then you can say whatever you want to her."

My heart was tight. I didn't want to come out of this place without doing the one thing I came here for. I came here to see Orena and that I was going to do, even though that meant stepping further inside Silvio's dominion, which wasn't something I was particularly fond of.

It was as if my body was moving like a ghost. One moment I was in the living room, the next I was in the kitchen, and the one after that I was in the courtyard. Before I knew it, I was standing behind a door and, on the other side of it, I was pretty sure that Orena was there.

The door opened, a nurse stepping out. She gave us a glance, but not much more than that. She was busy with whatever she was doing, which, I was certain, was making sure that the pregnancy was going to go perfectly. Nothing could go wrong, especially under Silvio's dominion.

"As you can see, I wasn't lying," Silvio joked, opening a huge smile.

Adamo still seemed ready to jump at him. If he tried something like that, I was ready to stand in his way. Nothing was going to ruin the peace in this place. Orena needed all the peace and quiet she wanted right now.

"How do we know you aren't lying?" Adamo asked. It was a genuine question, one that I could stand behind.

"I'm not." He took a deep breath, diverting his eyes from me. "I don't think we are even allowed inside the room. After all, it's a risky pregnancy. The doctors say that she wasn't ready for it when the contractions started."

My heart skipped a beat. Taking a step forward, I asked, "What do you mean? She was pregnant for so long. I think that it's about nine months since it started."

He lowered his head, shaking it. "I don't know the details. You're going to have to ask the doctors about that. What I told you is everything I know."

I fidgeted with my fingers, wishing that I was inside the room, but I was going to have to take Silvio's word for it. He said that she was in there and I had to trust him. After all, I just couldn't ruin this peaceful atmosphere, even though it was as if my life was spiraling out of control.

"I'm not so sure I can trust you right now," Adamo said, standing his ground.

"You have to. Otherwise, I don't even want to think about what might happen."

He tsked, lowering his eyebrows. I guessed that he was beginning to understand that his little row wasn't going to help anyone right now, especially Orena. I took one last look at the door, noticing that it had a small window.

I stepped toward it without asking for Silvio's permission. I feared he was going to put himself in my way, but he remained where he was.

He pulled up the side of his lips. "It looks like no matter what I tell you, you will never truly believe me, right?" And the way he said that, it was almost as if he was hiding something we should both know. Nevertheless, I didn't entertain the thought of what that might be.

If he was hiding something from us, then we were both going to find the truth out soon.

I stopped behind the small window in the door, peering through it and spotting Orena. She was lying on a hospital bed, with nurses and doctors around her. They were busy, sweat pooling on their foreheads.

I was happy that Silvio didn't lie, even though that didn't make me trust him more.

"Happy now?" He asked, but it wasn't a real question. Rather, he was trying to piss me off, even though it wasn't going to work. After everything that happened, when I thought I was finally going to fall in love with someone that wasn't Orena, she kicked me out of her life. I could never forgive her.

Since the night with Orena, I hadn't seen her. I wanted to see her again, though this time a little closer than where I was right now.

"She really is there," I murmured, spotting a couch by one of the sides of the hallway and sitting on it. When my ass sagged the soft pillowy material, Adamo ran up to the door, peering through the window.

"Orena…" He murmured, looking like a teenager right now. He looked like a teenager that had just fallen in love, which was interesting. It was the first time I was seeing true love.

He turned around slowly, sitting by my side on the couch. After minutes of silence without either of us saying anything, one of the doctors opened the door and crept his head through the gap. His eyes went from left to right and vice-versa, noticing that we were here.

His eyes locked with mine before he said, "She's ready to see you. Her baby is finally out, though she said that she didn't name him yet. And yes, that means that he is indeed a boy."

My heart raced. It couldn't be any more perfect. Orena didn't just deliver her baby, but he was also a boy. A baby boy. I wanted to hold him in my arms, even though he couldn't be my baby.

The doctor hurried out of the room, leaving us alone. I stood up the same moment that the other doctors and nurses left the room, leaving us completely alone with her.

It was quite weird that we were all going to be together in the same room with Orena. It was something that I thought would never happen again. I mean, I never even suspected that I would see her again.

When I stepped through the doorway, my heart sped up. Orena was still lying on the hospital bed, but this time she had a little bundle in her arms. It had to be the baby. The big, bright smile on her face confirmed that suspicion of mine.

She looked up, noticing that we were both going into the room. Whoever knew her when she lost her virginity to us wouldn't be thinking right now that she had all the right attributes to be a mother. Nevertheless, that's what she was. A mother.

"He's so beautiful. I'm so happy that I have him," she murmured and I didn't know what to do other than pulling up the chair and falling on it. I was the only one seated, the only one no more than two feet from her, and I knew that made the other guys jealous of me.

I held her hand, brushing my thumb over the underside of it. It was soft and smooth, just like the last time I touched it.

"I know," I murmured, letting go of her hand when I realized that Adamo was almost huffing over my neck. If he could do it right now, he would pull out his gun and shoot me. He was that obsessive and possessive when it came to Orena. I didn't know what happened between the two of them, but it was likely something deep, that was always going to remain in his mind, regardless of the consequences of what might transpire here.

But then, a huge and fat nurse came stumbling into the room, almost losing her balance. She planted her hands on her waist, glaring at us with mean eyes.

"You boys, I don't know what you think you're doing in here, but you aren't stupid. I think you can all see that she needs some rest, not to talk to anyone right now, and that you need to leave the room."

I glanced at Adamo and Silvio, noticing their sighs. "All right, you're completely right about that. We're interfering and we don't want to do that," Silvio lamented, glancing at us, which was his signal to make us both step out of the room.

That we did, but not before giving Orena one last look. She winked gently, which told me that she was okay with it.

It was a relief, I thought. At least, things were going to be okay, for now.

I guess.

ORENA'S EPILOGUE

I never thought I was going to become a mother and much less that my baby was going to come out without a name. This whole time, I didn't even ponder what name I should give to him. I didn't even know that it was a boy until things already spiraled out of control these last few months. My life was such a whirlwind that everything happened almost at the same time. One moment I was with Adamo, the next I was with Silvio, and then I was where I was right now.

Adamo was holding my hand. The tear coming out of his eye was telling. He never thought that he was going to get the answer he just ended up getting. Silvio was giving it in doses, almost as if he always knew the answer from the very beginning and was waiting to see what our reactions were like.

Even though I was letting Adamo hold my hand right now, it didn't mean that we were still a couple.

"You lied to me this whole time," I said, accusing him. It wasn't a true accusation as much as it was just me spewing out the truth. He knew that I was saying the truth, that what he did hurt me more than anything.

A moment of silence, nothing more than beeps of the machine filling the silence. I waited to see if he was going to say anything, but he was still just putting up a strong, firm expression on his face. He was always strong like that, unwilling to show weakness.

"I made a mistake and I'm going to own up to it. You just need to give me some time. I'm going to tell Magda about us and then we'll live happily together. That I promise you."

I pulled my hand back, realizing that it was pointless to go on with what he was saying. Not to mention that my current wishes were far bigger than just living the rest of my life with him.

I knew that the possibility was crazy and that, most likely, they weren't going to accept it, but I had to propose it anyway.

"Your promise isn't enough," I said, looking away, but soon realizing that Adamo wasn't about to give up. I was once someone who couldn't land a date with an average guy, and now I was where I was, with so many choices I was spoiled.

I could have Adamo, Silvio, and Gildo, but I wanted all of them at the same time. Was that something I could make happen? I didn't know, but I wanted to. I wanted to do a lot more than that, actually.

"What about the baby?" He asked, standing up and wiping the tear that was on his cheek. He looked a lot more resolute right now, which was impressive. I didn't think he could just will himself into looking tougher even though he just realized that he lost me.

Nevertheless, there was a way that he could have me as well again, even though I didn't think he was willing to share. "Shouldn't we give him a name?"

After a moment of silence as I pondered my answer, I said, "I want your input as well. I think that it's very important."

He snapped his head to me, widening his eyes. He opened and closed his mouth like he was a goldfish, which was funny and made me giggle.

"I mean it."

"What do you mean?" He asked, stepping toward me and then sitting back down on the chair. I checked him out from bottom to top, realizing that he was just as hot as before and especially when he was distraught.

It was still so terrible that we hadn't given the baby a name yet.

I mean, what was I waiting for? I guess, now that we didn't have anything else to worry about, the name was the only thing we had to concern ourselves with.

Adamo seemed confused, almost as if he thought this moment wasn't going to come. I didn't know for sure if that was what was going on in his head, but I felt some pity for him. Especially because now he had to dump his fiancée for me. It was the only way.

"Come here," I asked and he obeyed. He was right by my side again, letting my nose smell his perfume. It was strong, exuding his determination. "Do you already have a list of names?"

"A list of names?" He asked, grabbing my hand again and brushing his finger on it. He was doing that slowly, feeling the smoothness of my skin. Adamo wasn't going to give up on me just because I knew about his fiancée, right? "I don't have any."

"Well, we should come up with some. My mind is blank."

He cracked open a smile. "That isn't good. Someone like you, who always thinks of everything, should probably already have come up with several names."

I pulled my hand away. There was no point in giving him any signs that we could truly go back and become much more than what we were right now.

He scrunched up his eyebrows, showing me that he didn't like what I had just done. I took a deep breath, diverted my eyes to the door when I realized that a shadow just emerged behind it. For a moment, I couldn't make out who it was, but then it became obvious to me that it was Gildo.

We also still had a lot to talk about and he and Adamo were still enemies. So much so that their eyes flashed with anger when they noticed each other.

"What the hell are you doing here?" Gildo asked, clenching his hand. The anger pulsing out of his body was almost palpable. I could feel it all around in the room, impregnating it with its presence. "I thought that the nurse had said she shouldn't talk to anyone right now."

I figured that maybe we could all end up together, but now that time passed and I realized that nothing changed between the two of them, at least, maybe what I thought was nothing more than a pipe dream.

"I'm just making sure that she's okay. As you can see," Adamo said, spreading out his arms. "There's no nurse around and she isn't going to find out that we are here, as long as you keep your lips sealed."

Gildo didn't say anything, merely coming toward me before he asked, "How are you feeling right now? Hopefully much better than before."

Our eyes locked and I felt something flashing in them. I didn't know what it was, but I had a suspicion – that it was love. I never thought that someone like him was going to fall in love with me, but there it was. It was in his eyes, and in his lips, and in the rest of his body. I could feel it pulsing out of him.

"Yes, much better, thanks to Silvio," I said, realizing that that was something I thought I would never say. I never thought that I was even going to meet up with Silvio one more time.

After a moment of silence, Gildo asked, "So, what are we going to do now?"

Adamo narrowed his eyes. "What do you mean? I don't have to do anything with you."

Gildo sighed. "Don't behave like you are a child. Do I have to repeat myself?" He asked, clenching his hand.

"What did you just say?" Adamo asked, his voice growing deeper all of a sudden. He stood up slowly, making sure that Gildo knew he didn't take his words with kind ears.

Gildo shook his head. "Looks like I really have to say it with all the words."

"Just spew it out already. I was doing something important with Orena and I certainly don't have time for whatever it is that you are scheming."

"She isn't yours, Adamo. She isn't just yours. She's mine. She's

Silvio's, too, if you haven't figured that out yet. She's for all of us."

I bulged my eyes out. The last thing I thought I was going to be witnessing this morning was Gildo saying that he was willing to share me with them. I thought that, given that he was the only single man between the three of them, he wanted to keep me for himself only, but he thought differently. He had other plans in mind, and that made me see him with different eyes. Different, kinder eyes.

It was as though he just read my mind.

"Gildo…" I said and our eyes met again. They were sympathetic, coated with his love.

"It sucks that I had to say this in front of him, but the truth is that I love you. I thought I would never fall in love with someone I dated just once, but it happened and there's nothing that can be done about it."

I turned my eyes slightly to Adamo, realizing that he just unclenched his hand.

"I don't believe what I'm hearing right now. You want to take her from me?" He asked, rounding the hospital bed with the speed of a thunderbolt and grabbing Gildo by the collar of his shirt.

When he clenched his hand again and lifted it, I thought that they were going to fight, but I soon noticed that it was a misperception. Gildo grabbed his hand, pressing his fingers against it.

"You can punch me as much as you want, but it won't make a difference. You know that you want it as well, don't you? And you also know that it's the only way we can be happy. I thought about it for a very long time, thought that it was the only thing that could bring us together, and now I realize that I was right."

"So, what do you say we should do? That we should just…" Adamo trailed off, the words too hard for him to pronounce.

"That we should all be together?" A different voice asked, someone else stepping into the room. My eyes snapped to the right, finding him. It was Silvio. His gait was an easy one, his body moving as if he didn't weigh anything.

Everyone snapped their heads to him, finding him. Adamo let go of Gildo's shirt, stepping away from him. I was happy that at least, for now, they weren't going to fight.

"That suggestion is ridiculous. It's the first time I'm hearing it, and I'm not going to do that. Whatever it is that is going on in your mind, it's trash."

"I know it's difficult, but we can live here where everything is different. It's a different country, we don't even speak the language, and it's also where Orena will be welcomed with open arms. She could be happy here. Germany is an amazing country."

My heart pounded with happiness. I never thought that I was going to end up living in Germany, that I was going to settle down here, and much less that it was going to happen with three mafiosos.

What was even happening now?

Silvio turned his eyes, finding me. "But of course, we can't do that if she doesn't want it. That's why I have to ask you: do you want that too?"

The room fell in silence all of a sudden and I didn't know what to say. I pondered all the possibilities, everything that happened, and tried to predict the future. Doing so was difficult, almost impossible, but there was no other way.

I was just going to have to make some calls, tell my friends what was going to happen, but that was it.

I smiled softly. I guess I was really going to do that.

GILDO'S EPILOGUE

"So, are we really doing this?" I asked, standing in the middle of the living room with my nemesis. My enemies. We hated each other so much we thought that this moment would never happen, but here it was. We were together in the living room, holding glasses of wine.

"We should do it. It's the only way. After all, what's better for money making than establishing a monopoly in the market?" He asked, his eyes going from left to right, regarding all of us.

"You know what that means. Trying to establish a monopoly means going up against the government, who will become our biggest enemy. We won't be in America to fight against it and they will try to crush us."

Silvio gave us a snicker. "They can try whatever they want, but they know we are strong, especially together. When we are together, we can do anything."

I pulled up the side of my lips. Silvio wasn't usually right about anything, but he was spot-on about that. The government was going to think several times before acting against us. After all, they always relied on us remaining enemies for the rest of our operations in the country.

Now that we were banding together, things were going to be different. Cocaine was going to spread all over the country, infecting people's minds. Things were going to be glorious. I could already feel the money pouring into our bank accounts.

"I guess you're right," I said, lifting my glass of wine at the same time as they did, touching it against them. There was a clink that filled the room, our eyes meeting. Several things flashed between them.

And one thing was the fact that it was going to be tough leading our lives from now on. We were going to have to be watching each other's backs all the time.

We lowered our hands, tension filling the room. It was as though we were still talking, but only with our eyes this time. I supposed that it didn't matter that Orena was the thing holding us together. We were always going to be at odds against each other. We were always going to try to destroy the other.

I took another sip of the wine when I felt that someone was in the doorway. I turned around slowly, finding none other than Orena there. She was with her body resting against the door frame, regarding us with curious eyes. The smile on her face was gentle and soft, inviting me over to kiss her. It was such a pity that I couldn't, especially when Silvio and Adamo were with me.

I didn't mind angering them whenever I felt that it was justified, but I couldn't do that in front of Orena. She would suffer. She would cry and that was something I didn't want to witness.

"Look at you now. You were always at odds against each other, always trying to kill yourselves, but now you are working together. Or at least, that's what it looks like."

I chuckled, tipping the glass over my mouth and pouring all the liquid inside it. Feeling it as it went down my throat, I noticed how warm and good the taste was. It was almost like just being with Orena made the taste of the wine much stronger.

I stepped over to her, not thinking if maybe I was crossing a line. All I knew was that I wanted to be closer to her, to be holding her hand.

When I was so close to her I could feel the natural smell of her body, I asked, "Everything okay with our little one?"

"Yes, everything is okay with him." She averted her eyes to the right and then the left, continuing, "I want you to come with me to the nursery. There's something we need to talk about there, and it needs to be finished now."

I raised one of my eyebrows, but didn't question her about what it was that was in her mind.

"Whatever you need from us, we should go now," Adamo said, walking so that he was by our side. He was always so jealous and possessive of her that it made me question if our little arrangement was even going to work. Orena had to be strong so that this could work.

And she was going to be. If there was something I learned about her during our time together, it was that she was always strong.

Silvio was behind us, happy that we were now living in his house in Germany. Orena was in front of us and leading us. We crossed several hallways before reaching the nursery. Orena creaked the door open, leading us inside the room. When we were inside it, I couldn't help but stop where I was, turning my eyes from left to right slowly. Painfully slowly.

The nursery was perfect, colorful, and inviting at the same time. The walls were painted with a gentle, soft pastel tone. Toys littered the floor, the crib was big and spacious, and we even had a closed-off, fenced space where our little one could play when he was old enough.

It was dark, the moonlight streaking through the curtains. I flipped up the switch as I turned on the light. The light bulb came to life, illuminating the entire room.

Orena proceeded to the crib and I just noticed that she was holding a piece of paper in her hand.

She turned around slowly, looking at us. She waited until we were all in front of her and the crib.

"I don't want to know who the father of the baby is," she said, narrowing her eyes slightly. She was determined in what she just affirmed. It was surprising, but not entirely shocking. I figured she was going to say that.

Silvio, nevertheless, took a step toward her. His eyebrows were raised and his expression betrayed his shock.

"I don't get it. I went through so much and even got the DNA test results. I know that the baby isn't mine, but it could still be theirs," he argued, referring to us.

Orena shook her head gently. "I've thought about it this whole time and I've come to the conclusion that knowing that doesn't really matter. I don't want to know who the biological father of the baby is. It doesn't really matter. You are all family. You are all his fathers."

My heart started to race in empathy. I could feel where she was coming with that. It all made sense. If we didn't know who the biological father of the baby was, then it was one less reason to think that we couldn't work together. We still had the marriage, which was another thing we were going to figure out, too.

Some things were just left better forgotten, I thought.

Orena was then going to open her mouth again when Adamo stated, "I'm with Orena. I'm always going to do whatever she wants."

Except dumping his fiancée, I remembered. That was something he still needed to work on. He just needed a little nudge and then he would do that too, I figured.

Orena turned her eyes toward me, asking me the same question. And I had to answer by saying, "I agree. As much as it hurts me, there's no other way. It's better that we don't know."

Silvio was the only one against it, most likely because he was the one who kidnapped her and forced the DNA test on her. That was still something difficult to swallow. I still needed to confront him about it, and I knew that I eventually would.

Orena's expression softened up. She was happy that she got what she wanted, which was what was always going to happen. She was always going to get it, one way or another.

"And there's this one more thing we need to discuss," she said, reminding us that we still hadn't chosen a name for the baby. The more I thought about it, the more I realized how stupid that problem was. This whole time, we never took the time to think it through. "I've already chosen one, after getting your inputs. I took all of your inputs into consideration."

That was right. Some days ago, she was all over the house, looking for us and asking several questions. At the time, I didn't think much of them, but now it all made sense. All those things that I thought were unrelated, that didn't make much sense, were connected to the name of the baby.

"Well, what is it? What is the name of our little one?" Adamo asked, stepping toward her.

"It's Harry…" She responded and we all immediately went still. We didn't do that because we were shocked by the revelation, but because the name just made sense. Everything about it. It just resonated with the questions she made that time.

And, it was perfect. I couldn't imagine our little one with a different name.

SILVIO'S EPILOGUE

I was with my wife, looking down at her. Her eyes were slightly narrowed, but she understood that there was no other way. We were in front of my house in Germany and my children were with me, too. It hurt me the way it had to be done, but this was the only path to take. We didn't fight, didn't take this to be analyzed by a judge, and I still pulled it off. In the end, the boys thought that she was just going to take a long vacation.

In the meantime, I was hoping that they were going to get used to the fact that their mother wasn't going to be with us for a long time. By then, I hoped they would forget her, even though making that happen was going to be difficult. If I couldn't concretize that, then I hoped she would come and visit them as many times as needed.

"You know that this is the only way," I said, feeling a pang of pain in my heart. It didn't matter how many times I prepared myself for this occasion, it was always going to hurt me.

It didn't matter what my wife had to say to me right now. She couldn't. We talked about this many times before and already made up our minds about it. Not to mention that we couldn't argue in front of our children, anyway. They were behind me, a little curious about what was happening, but still oblivious to it.

"I know it is," she said, turning around and leaving. She went to the limousine that took her here, her hair flowing behind her head. She was still pretty the same way I knew she was, but I didn't have the same spark I once had for her. It was long gone and now I had a different one. It was with Orena, who was the love of my life.

I turned around, finding my boys. They were both wringing their hands, looking like they were twins. They were so cute and I just wanted to pinch their cheeks.

Quinto looked up, finding my eyes. Out of the two of them, he was the bravest. He knew when and how to ask the right questions, and even though I knew he was still oblivious to the full extent of what was happening, he was still going to prod the issue.

"Daddy, where's mommy going?" He asked and I grabbed his hand. It was small but warm. I wanted to be holding his hand for all of eternity. He wasn't used to being without his mom, but he soon was going to be. Especially when he started to interact more often with Often.

"She's going on vacation in Chile, like I said she was. I thought we already discussed this," I stated, holding his stare.

After a moment of silence, he blinked and then pulled up the sides of his lips.

"I trust you, daddy. It doesn't matter what happens, everything is going to be fine. I just know it."

"That's my boy," I said, ruffling his hair and then lowering my hand. I thought that he was going to figure out exactly what was happening here, but he didn't. That was a relief. I didn't want to admit it, but I was a shitty daddy. I should be stronger, but I always thought about their hearts when I considered telling them the truth. I supposed that it was better to wait until they were older and could better think about what was going on.

Bonifacio looked up, finding my eyes and then grabbing my hand. Then, he snapped his head to the left, finding something. I followed the direction his eyes were looking at and I figured out what it was. It was a small trampoline in the middle of the garden, where he could jump for as long as he liked.

He snapped his head back to his brother, saying, "Quinto, it's a trampoline! Don't you want to play in it with me? Let's go have some fun."

Before he said that, my heart was still a little upset, but now it was calm again. The environment around me was soothing. I couldn't hear anything more than the sound of the lawnmower cutting the grass. I could also hear some people talking in the distance, but they were nothing more than a distant noise that didn't mean much to me. It was all they were. Just noise.

I stood up slowly after crouching so that I could better talk to my son, hearing a pair of footsteps approaching me. My expression softened up when I realized that it was none other than Orena. She was alone, which was exciting. When she wasn't with the other guys, I felt a lot more comfortable around her.

"So, you finally grew a backbone," she said, putting one of her hands on her waist. Orena looked especially beautiful this morning. The light just seemed to bounce off her face in all the right ways, her curls falling gently around her face, and her lips crimson and full. To say that I wanted to make out with her would be far from the truth. I wanted to do a lot more than that.

"It was difficult," I said, settling a hand on her waist and pulling her closer to me. Our lips connected, our eyes closing. It was still difficult to wrap my head around the fact that I had to share her with the guys, but there was no other way around it. That was something I shoved into my mind a long time ago.

When we broke the kiss, she said, "I know. I know how difficult things are for you, but everything will get better. I promise that."

For a moment, I didn't say anything, just gazing into her eyes, admiring their color. They had the same color of honey, almost as if they also had the same composition. I brushed my finger over her cheek, kissing her one more time.

Changing the subject, I said, "And what is this perfume that you are wearing today?"

"I didn't think you were going to notice the change," she purred, her lips dangerously close to mine. I savored their taste, and it was exquisite. It made me want to kiss them for all of eternity, which was something that could happen, but wasn't. "You are so different now, especially after dumping your ex."

Orena and her didn't even meet up once. They never talked to each other and I preferred things that way. It was just better that way and also less complicated.

I brushed my finger under the underside of her lips, ignoring that we were surrounded by our bodyguards. I just heard the front gate of the estate opening, telling me that my wife might have seen us kissing.

But even if she did, it didn't matter.

I glided my hand down, cupping one of her asscheeks. Her skin was soft and gentle, and she let out a moan of pleasure. "Love, we shouldn't do this in front of the kids," she warned, locking her eyes with me one more time. I knew that we shouldn't, but I was still going to.

"How can I resist such a perfect ass?" I asked, pressing my body to hers, feeling her breasts pressed up against my chest. They were big and laden with her milk. She breastfed our baby every day. She was determined like that and loved the fact that it made her feel a little closer to our little Harris.

"You can always resist it, but you aren't because you aren't as strong as you think you are," she said against my lips, breathing slowly.

I turned my head left to right slowly, finding out that Bonifacio and Quinto were still jumping on the trampoline. I could hear their giggles from all the way over here. They were happy, exuberant giggles, and they made me want to be with them.

Nevertheless, something – or, rather, someone else – was keeping me from doing that. I pushed her forward with me and into the house, proceeding to the stairs. Orena then took the lead, swinging her ass gently left and right. She was teasing me and it wasn't fair. My dick was hard, harder than it was in a while.

When we reached the top of the stairs, my ears picked up the noise of car tires as a vehicle pulled over in front of the house. Peering outside, for a moment I thought that it was my wife coming back to say that she regretted everything, but then I realized that it was just Gildo and Adamo.

They came back from their meeting, which angered me. Just when I thought I was going to have Orena all for myself, they were already back.

ADAMO'S EPILOGUE

The room was dark, silent, and all I could hear was our slow breathing. I lifted my hand, undoing the first button of my shirt. Orena blinked once, focusing her attention on me. I undid the next button and then the next and the one that came after that. I didn't stop there, though, undoing all the buttons of my shirt. In no time at all, there was a gap between the two sides of my shirt, exposing my chest.

"You are always such a tease," Orena hissed, grabbing my tie and pulling me toward her, and making me fall on the bed with her. I was on top of her, my arms and hands on both sides of her body.

She was breathing slowly, her hands settling on my shoulders and then sneaking under the fabric. She roamed my skin and muscles with them as she took in how smooth and hard they were.

"You are such a beefcake," she murmured, puffing out her lips as she teased me again. She was teasing me that she was going to kiss me, but I knew that it wasn't the case. So much so that I didn't try to do anything afterward, just waiting for time to pass.

"And you are so beautiful. You are always beautiful and perfect," I said when she started to lower my shirt, revealing my torso for the delight of her eyes. They went up and down slowly, taking in what they were seeing.

I didn't like boasting about it, but my body was perfect and defined. One could look at it and think that I had almost 0% body fat, even though that was far from the case. It was certainly less than 10%, though.

After grabbing my shirt and bunching it in her hand, she tossed it to the side. It went past Silvio, who was still unbuttoning his shirt. I looked at his face as I groaned. I really didn't want to have to share her with him, but there was no other way.

The shirt fell on the floor as her hands started to explore my torso, feeling every curve and line. As she did that, I could see the rising levels of lust in her eyes. Her lips parted slightly, a cloud of breath coming out of them. I lowered my head as I attempted to cross a line, but then she raised her hand and pulled it against my lips.

My dick was rock hard. I wanted to be inside of her, to make love with her, which I was doing right now, but I also needed more.

She lowered her hand, saying, "I don't want you to kiss me now. Not before they can."

I groaned, but didn't let that phase me. In fact, I let her hands explore my chest, my shoulders, and my biceps. I wasn't even doing anything special right now, but my muscles were already flexing. They flexed under the touch of her fingers, reverberating with them.

"Why not?" I asked, moving my head so that I could kiss the side of her neck and before anyone could do anything about that. The other guys were still taking off their clothes. In the meantime, I was still dressed, but it wasn't an issue for me. Rather, it was the way I wanted this to play out. I was in a hurry to become her favorite one, which was something that was always going to happen. There was no way around it.

"It's just not fair. I don't want them to feel jealous of you," she responded, moving her hand under my pants, which made me laugh. I didn't think that they could ever get jealous of me, but okay. It was a legitimate concern.

"I don't care about what they think. All that matters is what you deserve," I said, putting my tongue out and flicking it over her lips. She closed her eyes, her lips parting before letting out a cloud of moan.

She moved her hand under my pants, groaning when she realized that I still had my belt on. "Let me get rid of this quickly," she announced, unbuckling my belt and then pulling it off. She tossed it to the side and I didn't turn my head to see where it went. All I heard was the rattle of the buckle.

I lowered my pants before she could do that, which earned me a smile from her. Before she smiled, though, she said, "You're always such a tease. I knew you were going to do that. We are going to have problems if you don't change."

"Keep doing what?" I asked, realizing that things were already rising to the next level and that I wasn't even inside of her. Not yet, anyway, but things still needed to be hurried up. I didn't want to compete against them until the time was right.

"You know what I'm talking about. You are the boss of your family, you are one of the most well-known criminals in the world, but here, in this house, I'm in control."

I smirked, knowing that she said the truth.

Nevertheless, I had little time to think about it. As soon as I was without my pants, Orena planted her hands on my ass. Digging her fingers in, she smiled devilishly.

"You are a little devil, aren't you?" I hissed, letting her do to my asscheeks whatever she wanted.

"It's just so good and warm. It makes me incredibly wet," she replied. Without my underwear, my cock was finally free. It was raging. Veins popped out over the surface, and one of them was thick and long enough to stand out from the rest. A bead of pre-come leaked out through the little slit. I was cut, my skin pulled back, and looking incredibly taught. My balls were heavy and tainted with a reddish color. My junk was just above her pussy and dangerously close to it.

I took a deep breath in, brushing the head of my cock against her slit. She shivered, her hands moving up until they were against the top of my back. When she reopened her eyes, they moved left and right and then up and down, studying my tattoos. It wasn't the first time that she was seeing them, but it was the first time that she could finally examine them like this.

"Something you want to ask me?" I asked, moving my hands so that they were under her thighs. I pulled them up until they were over my shoulders. Her little snatch was lined up to my cock and I was ready to penetrate her. I was going to do just so when I felt something heavy and hard hitting me on my shoulder. I fell over on the bed, realizing that that had been none other than Silvio. The evil smile on his face told me everything. He wasn't happy with what I did. He thought that I was going to take Orena all for myself, and he was probably right. I didn't want to share her, even though it was her wish.

We were nothing more than her pawns. Whatever Orena wanted, we needed to do it.

"It's my turn now," he said and I realized that Orena didn't mind what he just did. Actually, she smirked as if to show me that she was okay with that. It was preferable. The word itself hurt me. I wanted her all for myself.

He turned his head to her, pulling up her shirt and then removing it. He crumpled it in his hands and then deposited it on the floor, where it wasn't going to get in our way. He didn't have any clothes on now, his body shining under the moonlight coming through the window.

His hands went for her breasts, cupping them. His fingers moved around them and felt her skin for what it was. "It's incredibly soft and gentle," he said, making me feel even more jealous. But if there was a positive to take from that it was the fact that it made me want to exceed any expectations my queen had about me.

"And you are so incredibly hard right now," Orena muttered, moving her hand until she wrapped her fingers around his cock. It looked unbelievably tiny against his rod, which wasn't a pretty sight.

I didn't concentrate too much on it, instead focusing my attention on something else. Silvio was already on top of her, but that didn't mean I couldn't do anything I wanted right now. Actually, it was perfect.

Coming to that conclusion, I moved so that I was right behind her little cunt. It shimmered with the wetness coming out of it, her pussy lips slightly parted. I took a deep breath in, positioned myself better, and then thrust my tongue out.

I gave her snatch a long, powerful lick that made her body shiver. She looked down as she found me. The look on her face was revealing. She didn't think that I was going to be worshiping her cunt. My eyes went down and I found her clit. Her rosebud-like bundle of nerves was hard and enraged, poking out.

I winked and then gave her clit another lick. I made sure that it was hitting all the right spots and, then, I swirled my tongue around it, making it wetter. She shivered and I noticed that Silvio peeked over his shoulder. He was jealous of what I was doing, which was only making me feel more pumped up.

But then, he returned his attention back to her, mauling on her boobs. I wanted to be the one doing that, but it didn't really matter. I was doing something else that made me a lot harder than I was when we fucked her for the first time.

After giving her flower a couple more licks, making sure that it was lubricated, I repositioned myself so that my dick was against her entrance. I prodded it with my stick and then eased it in, breaking her initial defense. I noticed her hands gripping the bedsheets tightly. Her knuckles went white. It was the first time that I was seeing her like that. It was almost as if she was losing her virginity for the first time.

"It hurts," Orena hissed, but I knew she didn't want me to stop, and I didn't. I kept on sliding it all the way in, until I was at the end of her tunnel.

I gave her some seconds to get used to my size and it was

enough. When I was used to how much pressure she was applying with her walls, I started to roll my hips. Pounding in and out of her, I felt like I was already on the verge of exploding. And truth be told, I pretty much was.

Gildo didn't have much space, so he just stood by the side of the bed. Orena lifted her left hand and then she grabbed his rod. She started to shoot her hand up and down, pumping it. Against his cock, her hand was also unbelievably tiny.

In no time at all, Gildo threw his head back, rope after rope of come splashing against her pretty, chocolate-colored face. She loved every rope of come that hit her cheeks, her forehead, and even her lips. Orena wasted no time before sticking her tongue outside her mouth, licking up all of his white stuff.

"It's delicious. It's so tasty and salty," she muttered and after she finished saying that, I erupted inside her womb. She wasn't going to get pregnant. That much I knew, but it was still a special occasion.

I was the first one to cum inside of her this time, and I was always going to remember that.

We were all going to remember how much we loved Orena.

The End

The next page has a teaser for Impossible to Choose, another reverse harem romance. If that's what you're looking for, check it out. Lastly, leave a review if you liked this story. Thank you!

LOOKING FOR MORE BWWM REVERSE HAREM?

Impossible to Choose: A BWWM Mafia Reverse Harem Romance

Liana

Opening the door of the room, the first thing I noticed was that my father was absent. How odd. I thought that, for sure, he would be here. This time of the day, during the summer, he usually was here.

I didn't give that much thought, my mind going back to that college midterm I was going to take next week. I had so much to prepare for it, and I didn't know if I was going to do well. All I knew was that I was going to give my best.

And then, after that, I'd party. They were already planning out a party in one of the sororities, and I couldn't wait until I was there. I wanted to look good for one of the guys I had a crush on, or many of them. Choosing always was a difficult thing for me, and now was no different.

His office had an old-school look about it. The furniture, including the desk, the bookshelves, and the chair, was made of hardwood. The smell inside of it wasn't too bad, but it did remind me of an old library.

I did feel right at home here, though.

I'd come here looking for my father, but I still couldn't help but be curious. What was he hiding inside those drawers? If he was the kind of man I knew he was, then he'd surely have already locked-

And, it looked like that wasn't the case. That either meant I didn't know much about him, or that he just felt safe inside his home. He should be, considering the number of men he kept around. They usually carried guns with them, and they would do anything to stop someone from hurting one of my family members.

My sister should be, right now, in her room. She was younger than me and very annoying. As a teen, I supposed she wasn't much different from the others, but still... I couldn't stand her, especially because I thought she was too nasty. When was the last time she took a shower?

Here, in Miami, taking showers often was essential, after all.

I decided not to think more about her right now, focusing on looping two of my fingers around the handle of one of the drawers. Without requiring much force from me, I opened it and found a pile of documents inside.

I didn't think much of them until my eyes caught sight of a sentence that made my heart jump. Contract of Marriage.

Contract of Marriage – what?

That was the first thought that came into my mind. I didn't know anything about any wedding, and it certainly couldn't involve me. My family never mentioned marrying me to anyone. Not to mention - wasn't that something that happened in the past and not anymore?

I didn't give that much thought, trying to close the drawer and finding out that it just wouldn't go in at all. I pushed it with all of my force, and it was like there was a counter force preventing that from happening.

My eyes caught sight of something else, and it startled my mind. This couldn't be true. For sure, I was imagining all this and soon that was going to become evident. I was pretty sure that was what was going to happen.

Liana Hughes and Aleks Nikolaev. What in the world was happening here? This had to be some sort of mistake. I grabbed the sheet of paper and held it right in front of my eyes. I was imagining things. My name wasn't there.

And yet, it was. Unless I was imagining things or someone was playing tricks on me, this was indeed happening. My father had put my name on a contract of marriage, and it stated that I was to marry a Russian.

First, I didn't even know anything about him. I had my phone with me and, remembering it, I fished it out of the pocket of my pants and typed the name on Facebook. If that guy existed, then for sure he had an account there and I could find him.

Minutes later, I couldn't find his profile at all. I tried Instagram, Twitter, TikTok, and everything else I could remember, and I still couldn't find him. Whoever that guy was, he didn't appear to have any internet presence, which was puzzling.

I tried to calm myself down, but I soon found out that controlling my breathing was difficult. It was like a hand was squeezing my lungs, and I hadn't felt this anxious in a very long time. I usually brushed this sort of thing off, but this was the worst thing happening in my life in a very long time.

Ever since my boyfriend dumped me, I hadn't felt like this.

I opened my hand and let the sheet of paper fall to the floor. My hands were shaking, and I was still trying to figure out how I was going to approach my father about this. I needed to confront him about the wedding, and that wasn't even the beginning of it. I was going to put him up against a wall, and he would have to spill out everything.

My life… all of it was changing right in front of my eyes. I was going from a life where my biggest worry was studying for midterms and finals to getting married to a man I didn't know anything about…

Osip

My brother might be thinking that taking us to come to live

out here in the middle of nowhere was a good idea, but soon that was going to disappoint him. This was the first time I was stepping on foreign soil, and I hated everything about it.

I was standing inside the airport, marching forward with my brother. He was talking about how pretty his future wife looked, and I couldn't help but look at those affirmations with suspicion in my eyes.

Now, all of a sudden, he was showing interest in women?

His sexual orientation didn't matter to me one bit, but growing up, I'd always thought that he was gay, or felt ashamed of something about himself. I didn't know why he thought that marrying someone who wasn't Russian and from a powerful oligarchy family was a good idea, but there was no denying he got father behind the idea. Even he was supporting it.

Meanwhile, I was trying not to focus on those problems. If it weren't for our father needing us, I wouldn't be here as well. In fact, I'd be in Russia and skiing in the mountains. Man, I craved the snow and a place where the sun wasn't scorching hot. Even though the airport was supposed to have AC, I was still sweating like never before.

A necklace with a small cross hung from around his neck. He was walking with confidence, chin tipped up, and that was just like him. That was one of the reasons why, growing up, I couldn't bully him about not showing much interest in girls.

That was either something about him he didn't feel ashamed of, or he thought he'd been waiting for the right woman this whole time. Nevertheless, how could the latter be the case when he didn't even know the girl?

I didn't want to say this to him, but the whole thing was showing a side of him I never thought he had. He was desperate to marry someone and make it so our father chose him to become the next pakhan, right?

Well, at least the old man was going to wake up now with a smile on his old and decrepit face.

We were just rounding a corner when a shadow popped up in front of us. I stopped in my tracks and blinked twice. I couldn't have mistaken that person for another even if I was trying to. She was our sister, and I didn't think she was coming.

I mean, we had our estate here in Miami and it looked okay from the photos I checked out online, but still… I thought that she was going to remain in the motherland, doing whatever she did with her life.

"Wow, you really look alike," she exclaimed, pointing out the obvious. We were born almost at the same time, and it was still something that irked me a little. If I got a chance to make that different, I'd be doing so right now. It wasn't fair that I had to compete against Aleks all the time.

We talked for a little while, and we soon reached our mansion. Up close, the modernistic look was even prettier than on the photos, and I could already see myself living here for the time that Aleks thought he needed to be in the USA.

Then, as soon as that was over, we would move out of here and I would be able to return to doing the things that mattered the most to me.

I walked out of the mansion after the tour and hopped in my car. It was a red convertible, and it was perfect in a place that was so hot all the time. The sun was shining brightly behind me and I put on my shades after slicking my hair back with my hand.

I took off with just one destination in mind – that of meeting the wife of my brother. If he thought he could keep her looks hidden from me for long, he had something coming. Not to mention that he was more worried about his life problems, so he wasn't going to suspect anything about me not being in his estate anymore.

Driving through the city without knowing most of the ins and outs about it was painless. The roads were wide, the drivers behaved well for the most part, and the only annoying thing was all the tourists getting in the way.

I reached the place where she lived. It was also another walled-off estate. The guards in the front gate asked for my ID and made some calls, soon allowing me into the property when they figured out I was who I was saying I was.

The good thing about looking just like my brother was that most people thought we were the same person. That, I supposed, was one of the reasons why the guards allowed me in without double-checking my documents.

Not to mention that they looked afraid of me. They thought I would kill them if they didn't open the gate.

After rolling the car in and pulling over, one of the valets offered to park it somewhere in their estate. To be honest, I couldn't care much about what he did with it, as long as he left me alone. His hands were greasy and the smell coming from him was turning my stomach upside down...

Aleks

I told them I was going to wait to see her face for the first time during the wedding ceremony. Not before, and not after. But suffice to say that had been nothing more than a lie. I was standing in the middle of the party room, and I was spying on her.

Well, this was a masked party anyway. We were all wearing different masks to hide our faces. The party was happening in the estate of her father, who was talking with some business prospects on the other side of the room.

Her mother was sitting and laughing with her friends, unaware of my presence. I looked at those things with a smile on my face. Good. I had all the privacy and time in the world to speak with her.

We weren't allowed to take off our masks, and they did have openings at the mouths in case we felt like kissing. The environment inside the party was composed of a heavy and slow beat, guests dancing slowly, and people murmuring – even more so than they were talking about their issues.

I looked from side to side and couldn't find my brother. I didn't know what he was doing right now, but I would still know it was him even with a mask on. His gait and everything else about him – they were just like mine, and I would never mistake him for someone else.

Something about him – a memory – was nagging my mind again. I called him my brother and he looked just like me, but… in the end, that wasn't the whole truth. We didn't even have the same DNA. He looked a lot like me thanks to luck and factors I didn't have any control over.

My father was keeping that under wraps, and I'd always thought it was a terrible mistake. One other problem with that kept impeding me from telling him the truth. When it came down to it, despite all our differences, I loved him too much as the brother my father couldn't have given me without an adoption.

It still hurt me that I was keeping all of that hidden from him, but my hands were tied. I couldn't do anything else about it.

Our sister also didn't know anything about it. We had to continue keeping the secret, and I didn't think the truth would ever come out.

I pushed that thought out of my mind and focused on walking towards my bride. She didn't know that it was me and, until the wedding, she wasn't going to find out either way. I was planning on talking to her and getting to know her better.

After all, her father told me she was amazing and very beautiful. Nevertheless, I still needed to see the real Liana in person. That's why this party was happening. I set it up, and everyone else came.

She was all alone. I knew she had a small sister, her father, and her mother, but she didn't appear to have many friends talking with her. I didn't know if that was a common thing or not for her, but it kind of puzzled me anyhow.

She noticed my presence right away, turning around. As she did that, I registered all of the curves of her body. She was nothing short of beautiful. A sight for sore eyes, and she was making me wonder what kissing her would feel like.

She wouldn't be the first person I kissed. I wanted to marry her and build a family, but I wasn't the kind of man that saved himself for the right woman. I'd fucked plenty of them.

Last year, I slept with a dozen of them. Still, the problem I always came across was finding someone who stirred up something different in me. And, after looking at her photos and reading the reports my men wrote on her, it looked like she was the woman I'd always been looking for.

She opened a smile, and it looked like the most beautiful thing in the world. I couldn't deny that she was doing all sorts of right things in my body. My dick was stiffening, and I could only wonder for how long I could contain my temptations tonight.

Not to mention that she looked like the sort of person who could trust a stranger with ease.

"Hi, do I know you?" She asked, putting herself a little closer to me.

Liana was a bit on the chubbier side, and that only made her more beautiful to my eyes. I imagined myself bending her to my will, driving my cock deep inside of her, and filling her womb with my seed.

If someone were to be looking in my mind and reading all of my thoughts, they'd be saying I thought about sex all the time... and maybe they wouldn't be too wrong about that. After all, sex was always so good.

The only thing I wouldn't do tonight with her was that. I wanted to have Liana in my bed when I was married to her, and not before.

"We might, but in this party, we're not supposed to tell who we are. That's why I'm keeping that a secret..."

MORE BWWM DARK MAFIA AND OTHERS

SERIES ALPHA PREDATORS

1. Not my Wedding: A BWWM Dark Mafia Romance
2. Not my Vows: A BWWM Dark Mafia Romance
3. Not his Baby: A BWWM Dark Mafia Romance
4. Not my Fiancé: A BWWM Dark Mafia Romance
5. Not my Daughter: A BWWM Dark Mafia Romance

SERIES - PRETTY LIARS

1. Impossible to Choose: A BWWM Mafia Reverse Harem Romance

2. Kiss of Amnesia: Secret Baby BWWM Mafia Romance

3. Fake Boyfriend: Secret Baby BWWM Mafia Romance

4. A Baby for the Hitman: Secret Baby BWWM Mafia Romance

5. Mafia Boss's Surrogate: Amnesia BWWM Dark Mafia Romance

Other dark mafia romances:

Beg Me: An Arranged Marriage Dark Mafia Romance

Used by the Mafia Boss: A Dark Mafia Romance

Bait Me: A Dark Mafia Romance Bundle

Mafia Vassal: A Dark Italian Mafia Romance Bundle

Don't Cry: A Secret Baby Dark Mafia Romance

Seizing her Heart: A Bratva Mafia Romance Collection

Conquering my Queen: A Dark Mafia Romance Bundle

ABOUT THE AUTHOR

Ruthless mafiosos, gorgeous billionaires, and feisty heroines are just tiny fractions of Jolie Damman's stories. She breathes and lives dark romance, peppering each scene with intrigue and tension that sweep readers away.

A kiss isn't just that. When a characters' eyes meet another's, they speak of memories even they can't understand. It might hurt. There might be triggers, but it's all worth it in the end, and that's what Jolie Damman always believes.